TAFT 2012

A novel

By Jason Heller

QUIRK BOOKS

PHILADELPHIA

Library of Congress Cataloging in Publication Number: 2011933458

ISBN: 978-1-59474-550-8

Printed in Canada
Cover design and illustration by Doogie Horner
Cover photo by Sherwood Forlee
Interior design by Katie Hatz
Production management by John J. McGurk

Quirk Books
215 Church Street
Philadelphia, PA 19106
quirkbooks.com

10 9 8 7 6 5 4 3 2 1

To the real Irene: Margaret Smith, my grandmother, who came into this world the same week Taft was voted out of office. I hope you're somewhere fixing a nice plate of chicken-and-dumplings for Big Bill right now.

PROLOGUE

"THE BIGNESS OF THE JOB demands a man of Taft's type. He is thoroughly prepared for the task.... Never has there been a candidate for the Presidency so admirably trained in varied administrative service. Creed and color make no difference to him; he seeks to do substantial justice to all. There isn't a mean streak in the man's make-up. No man, too, fights harder when he thinks it necessary—but he hates to fight unless it *is* necessary."

—*President Theodore Roosevelt, explaining why he endorsed William Howard Taft to follow him in office, 1908*

"To be a successful latter-day politician, it seems one must be a hypocrite.... That sort of thing is not for me. I detest hypocrisy, cant, and subterfuge. If I have got to think every time I say a thing, what effect it is going to have on the public mind—if I have got to refrain from doing justice to a fair and honest man because what I may say may have an injurious effect upon my own fortune—I had rather not be president."

—*President William Howard Taft, two years into his term, 1910*

December 6, 1912

Dear President Taft.

I am sorry you lost your election. My daddy says Wilson is a lousy so & so. When you are not busy being President any more you can come visit me at my house because I am from Cincinnati too. I would like a Teddy Roosevelt bear for Christmas. Thank you for reading my letter. Liberty & justice for all.

Signed, Irene O'Malley, age 6

==

The Washington Herald
Editorial column
March 5, 1913

The *Herald* editorial board would like to add a final note to our exclusive reportage of President Wilson's inauguration.

This newspaper has certainly had its disagreements with William Howard Taft during the four years he resided at 1600 Pennsylvania Avenue, and we have not hesitated to point out the many occasions upon which "Big Bill" failed to live up to his predecessor Mr. Roosevelt's fine example: for instance, his shameful treatment of that American institution, U.S. Steel. His refusal to sign legislation that would have sensibly restricted immigration to the literate. His un-American love for taxing businesses at the exorbitant rate of *an entire percent* of their annual income. This editorial board could go on at length!

But, for all these faults, we must acknowledge that Mr. Taft usually managed to approximate the personal behavior of a civil gentleman while president, a fact that leaves us all the more scandalized by his behavior yesterday. After saying his good-byes at the White House door in the morning, Big Bill subsequently did not bother to *show up at all* for resident Wilson's swearing-in. A more egregious snub, a more unpresidential breach of propriety, can hardly be imagined!

Thus, having been granted no opportunity for a final interview with the twenty-seventh president of the United States—and, we might point out, the tenth president to be denied a second term by an unhappy American people—the *Herald* editorial board must deliver our parting words here upon this page: Shame on you, Mr. Taft. We surely don't know what errand you could possibly have found so much more important than handing the reins of American democracy to your successor. Did you imagine Ohio could not wait another twenty-four hours to have its "biggest success" back? Or could you simply not bear to face a crowd of 250,000 people most eager to cheer your victor?

In any case, we have no doubt that the American people will see Big Bill again soon. After all, how could we *fail* to see him? The man is so large, he had to be pried loose from the White House bathtub. A proud legacy indeed, sir.

PART I
2011

ONE

DARK.
It had been dark for so long. Dark and warm and wet and heavy. And silent.

So silent.

But not entirely so. He could hear things sometimes. A low hum of machines. A distant peal of laughter. A soft patter of either rain or tears.

He could feel things, too. The settling of the soil. The tickle of roots. The stately migration of the seasons.

And hunger. Good lord, the hunger.

He gnawed at the loam sometimes as he dreamed. He imagined he was buried under an avalanche of roasted chicken and brown gravy and custard. All he need do was eat his way out.

Instead, he slept.

That is, until the lights came.

It was a twinkling at first. They flashed intermittently, these lights, and then they quickly disappeared. He felt the dull thud of concussion, too, but knew not from where. But each flash and each thud brought him, bit by bit, out of his slumber.

Damnation, was he hungry.

With the hunger came memories. They lasted only as long as the flashes of light. First was a vision of a woman. A thin, pale woman. She spoke with difficulty, but she was happy, and she was strong-willed and alive. Even from this distance of space and time and consciousness, he drew from that strength.

Then there were children. Small ones and grown ones. There was a house, white as though carved from ivory. There was a man: bespectacled face round and beaming, voice so much louder than his own.

Then there was a smell. O glorious smell! The memory of it alone was almost enough to quell his ravenous, belly-clawing hunger. It was cherry. Cherry blossoms. The specter of the cool, sweet scent crept across his soul like a song. It came and went, but each time it faded, he clutched at it as if it were his own life's blood.

Then, one day or minute or millennium later, he didn't simply dream of the cherry blossoms. He smelled them.

The scent washed over him as he bolted upright. Other smells filled his nostrils too: rain and smoke and the familiar tang of roses. The cherry was faint, but it was there.

He had to find it. He ignored his hunger, ignored his pain, and pulled himself out of the infernal pit in which he'd found himself. He knew he was slathered in mud. No matter; he'd had mud slung at him before.

Groaning, his voice horribly coarse, he staggered into the light rain, looking for his beloved cherry blossoms. But there were none. It was autumn. The blossoms were long gone.

So instead he ran toward the sanctuary. The place where his one true friend slept.

The fountain.

But before he could make it there, he heard screams. He answered them in kind. He kept running.

That's when he heard a crack like thunder and felt a fire like lightning in his leg.

He fell. His waking dream had passed.

When he woke again, water was running down his face. He could feel it stripping the mud from his skin and dripping from his mustache. He looked up. Hovering over him were men and women with brightly lit machines perched on their shoulders.

In the distance, a man ran toward them. He held what looked like a gun. He opened his mouth. Words came out.

"Hey, turn off those cameras! Back away! Oh, my God—that face. That's impossible. Holy shit."

CLASSIFIED
Secret Service Incidence Report
WHG20111107.027
Agent Ira Kowalczyk

At approximately 1042, an oversized mammalian figure covered in mud appeared behind the White House South Lawn Fountain, approaching the press conference in progress on the lawn. It was unclear to me for several seconds whether the intruder was a man or a large animal as it lurched toward the crowd while moaning loudly. As the closest perimeter guard, I drew my firearm and ordered the intruder to halt while the executive guard secured POTUS. The intruder bellowed louder and attempted to proceed past the South Lawn Fountain in the direction of POTUS and the press corps. I discharged my weapon once, striking the intruder in the leg, and he collapsed against the fountain. I approached and saw that the water from the fountain, along with the morning drizzle, was washing the mud from the intruder's body. He was a very large man, over 6 feet tall, probably 300 pounds, wearing a formal tweed suit. He had white hair and a handlebar mustache. My first thought was that he looked like some sort of deranged presidential history buff dressed up as William Howard Taft.

From *Taft: A Tremendous Man*, by Susan Weschler:

I'll never forget the moment I first saw him on the television screen. Not a picture—*him*. There was no mistaking him. I'd been studying the history of the man who owned that plump, jowled, puffy-eyed face my entire professional life:

Taft.

William Howard Taft. Twenty-seventh president of the United States. Weighed in at 335 pounds. Worked with unceasing devotion to the job for four years—but was so honest a politician, he ended up infuriating every single interest group that had ever supported him. Lost his 1912 reelection bid in a miserable, crushing defeat. And then just *disappeared* the morning of March 5, 1913, the day his successor, Woodrow Wilson, was inaugurated. Taft was never seen or heard from again; his last known words, spoken right outside the White House just hours before Wilson took the oath of office, were: "I'll be glad to be going. This is the loneliest place in the world." After that sad utterance, Taft never showed up for the ceremony. Or anything else. Ever.

Which meant the chaotic footage they kept replaying on CNN couldn't be real. Couldn't be him. How could he be here now, a century later, stumbling mud-covered into the midst of an unsuspecting White House press conference?

And yet that was clearly no fake girth, no Halloween mask. It was either the oddest terrorist attack in history, the stupidest reality-show prank imaginable . . . or it was Taft.

Like some sort of jolly were-walrus, he sat on the edge of the South Lawn Fountain, blinking and grinning. He was still filthy, but the rain had finally uncovered most of the man. He wore a great wool overcoat, a suit so stuffed that it strained at the buttons, and a huge filthy mustache that swirled and twirled and bristled across his upper lip. Beneath his feet, the water of the fountain had turned faintly red. He appeared to be in shock—and then he spoke. His voice was much higher and more melodious than you'd expect from such a giant of a man as he uttered the words that now live forever in the annals of history: "I will gladly grant a Cabinet position, of your choice, to the first upright citizen who brings me pudding cake and a nice lobster thermidor." Then, of course, he collapsed.

TWO

H E HAD SLEPT, and woke, and slept again. Doctors had come and gone. So had men in black suits. Both had asked a great many questions. One or the other had drawn blood from the crook of his elbow and even had the unmitigated gall to clip a bit of hair from his mustache. The hair had been quickly sealed in a small transparent bag, but he felt scarcely strong enough even to wonder what that was all about, much less ask. Through it all, peculiar electrical devices whirred and pinged, and he faded in and out of consciousness.

Finally, after his third or fourth doze, he sat up, lucid, hungry. Alone. He was in a well-appointed bedroom suite; under the bed sheets, he was naked and clean. Draped over an armchair lay a fresh gray suit that looked to be close to his size, though for some reason it included neither waistcoat nor hat. He climbed out of bed and found that the suit was impeccably tailored, but it was still difficult to squeeze into, particularly his left leg, the upper half of which was swathed in an ungainly bandage.

Taft didn't recognize the room, but he knew the smell of the place. It had filled his nostrils much as it had saturated his soul over the past four years.

He was in the White House.

No sooner had he spit-shined his shoes and curled the ends of what remained of his mustache, a knock came at the door.

"Yes, by all means, come in!"

The door creaked open, and a tall, thin man in a suit—*also* missing its waistcoat!—walked in. He crossed the room, smiled, and offered Taft his hand.

"Mr. Taft, please. Don't try to get up. You've been through a lot in the last twenty-four hours."

"It appears I have! And who might you be? Are you here to bring me my meal? You will be my eternal hero if you could run down to the kitchen and fetch me a ham or two."

The man closed his eyes for a brief moment before smiling again. "Dinner will be coming soon. First, I need you to listen. It may not seem like you were sleeping for long, and Lord knows we have no idea how or why this happened. But you went missing from the White House . . . quite some time ago. This is not exactly the world you remember."

Taft laughed. "Not the world I remember? Why, I'd have to agree with you there. Today I've been shot, assaulted with strange machines, and spoken to in riddles. I appear to be in a world where the president of the United States can be condescended to like a child. By a manservant such as yourself, no less."

"Mr. Taft," the man said, "I need you to keep an open mind here, today and in the coming days. There is a lot you're going to need to adjust to. First of all, I am the president of the United States. Not you. Not Woodrow Wilson. Me."

Before Taft could counter him, the man raised his hand and pressed on.

"You've been missing and presumed dead—one of America's great mysteries—for a *very* long time. Don't worry, the United States is still strong, still proud, still prosperous. But—" He hesitated. "Well, I'd better just say it. You've apparently been asleep for almost ninety-nine years. Today is November 8. The year is 2011. Mr. Taft, welcome to the twenty-first century."

PAULINE CRAIG: A giant beast of a man bursts into a presidential press conference, is shot by Secret Service, and now, two days later, the White House is telling us that this befuddled intruder in a carnival mustache *really is* the missing former president William Howard Taft. Almost a hundred years after he vanished. I'm used to the government telling whoppers, but come on, now! Well, one way or another, it's history in the making, folks. You're living it. And *Raw Talk* is here to break it all down for you. Our first guest today, with us via satellite, is Director of National Intelligence James Mackler. Director Mackler, you've come on *Raw Talk,* much to our amazement, to back up the president's outrageous claim earlier today that the man who stumbled onto the White House lawn has turned out to be the real William Howard Taft.

JAMES MACKLER: Thank you, Pauline. Under normal circumstances, an ongoing national security investigation wouldn't be something we'd publicly comment on so quickly. But with Monday's bizarre incident happening live in front of cameras, and—and with the startling facts we've uncovered, the president wants to get the information out to the public as quickly as possible, to minimize confusion and head off any worries about possible terrorist threats. So, here it is. Let me first explain—there are many levels of government security. There's secret, and then there's top secret—

PAULINE CRAIG: And then there's SCI, sensitive compartmented information, which is the very highest top secret.

JAMES MACKLER: Yes. We compartmentalize the most extreme federal security information. And in the very smallest compartment—the information that, until now, no one outside the tightest, most secure handful of officials has even needed to know even existed, much less known what it is—is the identification code every president since the Civil War has memorized to protect the government against infiltration by a presidential impostor.

PAULINE CRAIG: In case something like—well, something like this happens.

JAMES MACKLER: Yes. It's never happened before. No president's identity has ever been called into question, until two days ago. We asked our apparent Taft for the presidential ID code. He knew it.

PAULINE CRAIG: He knew it. I see. And you're more prepared to accept the idea of a total violation of the laws of nature than the idea that a government secret could have leaked.

JAMES MACKLER: There are secrets, and then there are *secrets*, and then, beyond those, there are the secrets so secret they keep secrets from each other. I don't know how to explain his appearance after a hundred years, but I do know as an absolute certainty that that man could not know that code unless he used to sit in the Oval Office.

PAULINE CRAIG: Well, let's ask our second guest, also here via satellite: Dr. Ernest Cho, chief biologist at the Naval Research Laboratory. Dr. Cho, the intelligence community IDs this man as William Howard Taft. What does science have to say about the fact that it's impossible?

ERNEST CHO: Pauline, I know this is all incredible, but—we've got two things to address, the *if* and the *how*. The if is pretty straightforward: the Smithsonian collection has vintage samples of President Taft's hair. We spent yesterday running a DNA test, and it was a match. Genetically speaking, that man is either William Howard Taft or his brother. And, of course, his brothers have been dead and buried for a century.

PAULINE CRAIG: Well, gee, are you sure about that?

ERNEST CHO: Ah, yes. We've—we've checked. Sorry, I know that's unpleasant, but there's no room to be sloppy with something like this. On top of the DNA, every physical identifying trait also matches President Taft's medical history, which is well documented. His wife was obsessed with his health. There are a *lot* of records. As for how he could have vanished for a century and still be not only alive but unaged—we don't know. Ah, there are certain hunter-gatherer tribes in New Guinea that are able to arrest the human metabolism by absorbing a mixture of arboreal fungi, but nothing that approaches this magnitude. Mr. Taft, for his part, has no sense of time having passed whatsoever. He tells us he thought he'd just sat down outside and dozed off while walking to Woodrow Wilson's inauguration.

PAULINE CRAIG: In 1913.

ERNEST CHO: Yes. There certainly have been cases of human hibernation reported occasionally throughout history. They're far-fetched, obviously, and science is reluctant to accept the truth of things that cannot be explained. But every scientific tool we're able to apply to this situation tells us that, this time, the far fetched is true. He's Taft.

PAULINE CRAIG: Human hibernation. Well, if any human was going to hibernate, I guess it makes sense that it would be one who looks like a bear. Our final guest is preeminent Taft historian Susan Weschler of American University. Professor Weschler, you've been working on a biography of President Taft for years. Would you say you know him better than anyone else living today does?

SUSAN WESCHLER: Uh, thank you, Pauline, that's very kind. I suppose that's true. But being the foremost authority on Taft is like being the foremost authority on—on Luxembourg.

PAULINE CRAIG: I don't follow you.

SUSAN WESCHLER: Luxembourg is a tiny little nation surrounded by Germany, Belgium, and France. It's overshadowed by its more powerful, more popular neighbors, so people never give it any thought. Taft is like that. His term was sandwiched right in between Theodore Roosevelt and Woodrow Wilson, two of the most exalted presidents we've ever had.

PAULINE CRAIG: I've seen Taft, Professor, the pictures as well as the man on the White House lawn Monday. And I have to tell you, he's no tiny little Luxembourg. Though I'm sure he does know about sandwiches.

SUSAN WESCHLER: Pauline, if you invited me onto your show just to crack fat jokes—

PAULINE CRAIG: Settle down, Professor, just a little humor to break the tension.

SUSAN WESCHLER: I'll tell you this. Give me an hour with that man, and I'll know whether he's William Howard Taft.

JAMES MACKLER: Professor Weschler, I expect you'll get that chance.

PAULINE CRAIG: Director Mackler, how will President Taft's reappearance affect the political landscape? How does it change the dynamic of the 2012 election?

JAMES MACKLER: I hardly think that's on anyone's mind right now.

PAULINE CRAIG: I hardly think it's *not*. Unfortunately, President Taft's great-granddaughter, first-term Ohio Congresswoman Rachel Taft, declined our invitation to come on the show today. Has the congresswoman spoken with her ancestor yet?

JAMES MACKLER: Congresswoman Taft is in Mexico right now with a trade delegation. The president has been in touch with her about the situation.

PAULINE CRAIG: Mark my words, America: if a Republican president from the past is back on the scene, his granddaughter in Congress just got a whole lot more interesting. We'll be back after these messages.

FROM THE DESK OF REP. RACHEL TAFT
(Ind.–OH)
To-do list—Wed. 9th

—Tour three more agricultural facilities in Santiago de Querétaro

—Prep for debate over provisions of International Foods Act

—Charity lunch for orphanage in San Miguel

—Phone conference with staff about budget-tightening measures

—Remind Trevor to pick up birthday cake for Abby

—Figure out what the *hell* is up with man who appears to be resurrected great-grandfather

THREE

A S CHIEF EXECUTIVE and commander-in-chief of the United States of America, William Howard Taft had been privy to many secrets. Some were trivial. Others were earthshaking. Many, he cringed to recall, still pressed heavily on his soul.

But as he sat in an unnaturally comfortable chair in one of the West Wing meeting rooms—which was now, he marveled, equipped with an incomprehensibly begadgeted conference table—there was one secret above all that he wished he knew: how in thunderation did they get the meringue inside of these little yellow cakes?

"What manner of witch *is* this Hostess?" he mumbled, putting down the plastic wrapper and peering at the creamy end of one of the half-eaten pastries. These so-called Twinkie cakes were the cap to the fine, sprawling meals the White House kitchen had been serving him the last two days. A couple of his favorite recipes had proven to be somewhat archaic, just as that Secret Service fellow, Kowalczyk, had warned him. But in the end the intrepid chefs had persevered by consulting an unseen scholar the agent had called

Goggle or Google or something to that effect. God bless this encyclopedic Mr. Google, whoever he was.

With his stomach near to bursting, Taft's mood had likewise resumed its full capacity. His mind, though, was still quite a bit hazy—no doubt thanks to the pills the White House physician had been giving him since removing the bullet from his leg. But he'd warily palmed the last two tablets and slipped them into his pocket, and he'd begun at last to clear the cobwebs and gather the rudiments of his memory.

All he could put together were bits and pieces. Flashes of Cincinnati. Fragments of the Philippines. The stout, sober face of his aide-de-camp and best friend, Major Archibald Butt. The wooden grimace and bad teeth of his victor in the 1912 election, Woodrow Wilson.

Wilson. He remembered the man's Inauguration Day, barely. His own last day in the White House. With his head in a cloud of melancholy thicker than the thunderheads that had suddenly marred the bright day, he had wandered into the rain to escape the pomp and circumstance of the coming ceremony. The storm had seemed to descend from the sky and enfold him, calm and warm, like having the eye of a hurricane all to oneself. Suddenly exhausted, he'd lain down in a soft, warm, wet spot, some garden or another on the Ellipse. Content at last to let go of the pressures and stresses and relentless scrutiny of his office, he slept.

And then he'd woken up. Here. Now.

It was all so incredulous. Still, he was a rational man. Perhaps it was merely a suggestible demeanor brought on by the pills he'd been given, but there was no doubt in his mind that he must indeed be in the future. This was too elaborate to be a hoax pulled off in the White House. And the taciturn Woodrow Wilson was hardly the joking type.

But it was neither Wilson nor Butt whose memory gnawed at the very core of Taft's spirit. There was something or someone else—a soul so intimately tied to his own as to be invisible in its pervasiveness—that he couldn't quite put his finger on. At first he recalled a touch, so brittle yet so strong. And then a gaze, gray and infinite. And then that scent again, the sweet, faint, tantalizing tang of cherry blossoms—

His reverie was interrupted by his new bodyguard, Agent Kowalczyk, clearing of the throat. "Sir, you okay over there? You look a little out of it."

"Hmm? Out of *what*, exactly?"

"Out of . . . ah, never mind." Kowalczyk folded his shiny black device—it looked like a tin of lozenges—and slid it into his pocket. "Just making sure you're feeling okay. After—you know—I, um, shot you."

"Again I say, don't fret over it. I'm embarrassed to have collapsed from such a glancing scratch. A bullet is naught but a glorified pebble. Why, a worthy opponent of mine once delivered a campaign speech just moments after being shot by some lunatic in Milwaukee. *He* didn't let himself be stopped by some paltry slug." Taft frowned. "Now, why for the life of me can't I remember who that was . . ."

Just as quickly as he had regained his good cheer, he'd become troubled once more. But it wasn't because of the agent's handwringing. A swift and spine-tingling chill lanced through Taft's body. "Kowalczyk, tell me," he said with a rippling shudder. "What room are we in exactly? I should know, but I don't."

"What room? Oh, right. Things have probably been rearranged in the White House since you lived here. This is the Roosevelt Room. He built the West Wing, didn't he? But it didn't get named that until the '60s, I think."

Roosevelt. The name flashed like lightning inside his skull. Theodore Roosevelt. His predecessor. His mentor. His friend. His greatest supporter, and then, later, his most terrible adversary. A man whose smaller yet somehow grander frame had always cast a shadow over Taft.

But Roosevelt, he knew, must be long dead now. Dead like Woodrow Wilson. Dead like his children.

Dead.

Like Nellie.

Taft dropped his snack cake as he felt a tightening in his chest. No, not a tightening. A clenching, as if the centuries themselves sought to rip his heart from his breast and send it hurtling back to its rightful place, its rightful time.

Its rightful owner.

Through a halo of pain and anguish, Taft heard Kowalczyk yell for the doctor. But Taft was already halfway out the door. Like an enraged beast—the kind Teddy used to make headlines shooting while on safari—he threw open the door of the Roosevelt Room and charged into the hallway, seeking only escape.

Then he crashed into some other body and went down in a tangle of limbs.

Hands pushed him. Arms pulled him. He unleashed a howl from the pit of his being. Like a tortoise rolled onto its shell, he found himself suddenly on his back.

Next to him on the floor lay his wife.

"Nellie! My dear, oh, my dear." His tears came in torrents. "I thought you were gone, too. Oh, my Nellie. I thought you were gone."

As he pawed at his eyes, though, his vision came back into focus. This woman he'd collided with was small and slim like Nellie. She had the same serious look on her face, a fetching expression of certain, quiet determination.

But she wasn't his beloved. She wasn't his wife.

She wasn't his Nellie.

"President Taft," the woman said awkwardly. "Ah . . . there now. It's all right. It's going to be all right."

Taft, his head buried in his chest and his sobs coming in gasps, felt thin, cool arms around him.

"Mr. Taft, please. Take a breath. Deep breaths, okay? Good. Are you all right now? My name is Susan. Susan Weschler. It's an honor to meet you, sir." Then the arms gripped him tighter. "Oh, you poor man."

Fox News Poll

If the election were held today, would you vote to reelect the president or vote for an unspecified Republican challenger?

Reelect the president: 43 percent
Unspecified Republican challenger: 47 percent
Undecided: 10 percent

From the official White House biography of former First Lady Helen "Nellie" Taft:

As "the only unusual incident" of her girlhood, Helen Herron Taft recalled her visit to the White House at seventeen as the guest of President and Mrs. Hayes, intimate friends of her parents. The fourth child of Harriet Collins and John W. Herron, born in 1861, she had grown up in Cincinnati, Ohio, attending a private school in the city and studying music with enthusiasm.

The year after this notable visit she met "that adorable Will Taft," a tall young lawyer, at a sledding party. They found intellectual interests in common; friendship matured into love; Helen Herron and William Howard Taft were married in 1886. A "treasure," he called her, "self-contained, independent, and of unusual application." He wondered if they would ever reach Washington "in any official capacity" and suggested to her that they might—when she became Secretary of the Treasury!

No woman could hope for such a career in that day, but Mrs. Taft welcomed each step in her husband's: state judge, Solicitor General of the United States, federal circuit judge . . . [and] Secretary of War. His election to the presidency in 1908 gave her a position she had long desired.

As First Lady, she still took an interest in politics but concentrated on giving the administration a particular social brilliance. Only two months after the inauguration she suffered a severe stroke. . . .

The capital's famous Japanese cherry trees, planted around the Tidal Basin at her request, form a notable memorial. . . . Retaining to the end her love of travel and of classical music, she died at her home on May 22, 1943.

You're listening to C-SPAN Radio. *We now go to the Dirksen Senate Office Building on Capitol Hill for a live press conference with Massachusetts Republican senator Sean Brown of the Senate Committee on Homeland Security and Government Affairs, where a hearing earlier today determined that ex-president William Howard Taft is entitled to a federal pension. We join the event already in progress.*

REPORTER: Senator, legal experts have suggested that if Mr. Taft is grandfathered into coverage under the Former Presidents Act, the government will be forced to grant him his pension back pay retroactively for the ninety-nine years since he left office. Isn't this a hugely wasteful expenditure?

SEN. BROWN: It would be if it were true. Fortunately, it's not true. I'm surprised that wasn't made absolutely clear during the hearing. The committee has agreed with the General Services Administration that since Mr. Taft did not apply for coverage at any point before now, his pension and benefits will begin from their initial term of service this month.

REPORTER: Senator, these benefits include a two-hundred-thousand-dollar-a-year pension, a hundred-thousand-dollar annual budget for staff, an office, and a full-time Secret Service guard. Can you state, for the record, what's the responsibility of a former president to continue qualifying for these benefits?

SEN. BROWN: The responsibility? I'm sorry, can you elaborate?

REPORTER: What does the former president have to give back to the American public in exchange for this ongoing compensation?

SEN. BROWN: Well—wow. I think the idea inherent in "former president" is that he's *already* served the American public at the very highest level of commitment. A former president doesn't need to requalify every year—he's in the history books forever, you know? Next question.

REPORTER: Senator, Mr. Taft will also be eligible to receive top medical care at VA hospitals. Doesn't it set a bad example to allow him the same treatment as our veterans when his extreme obesity makes him a clear insurance risk? Will the First Lady's anti-obesity campaign be addressing the matter of President Taft's physical fitness?

SEN. BROWN: I'm not going to answer that question. Thank you, that will be all.

CLASSIFIED
Secret Service Incidence Report
BBO20111114.134
Agent Ira Kowalczyk

At 0535, formally assumed command of guard detail at the secure 7th & E Street apartment location, now designated Big Boy One. Big Boy scheduled to move in at 0630. Prof. Weschler scheduled to arrive at 0900 for full security briefing before assuming position as special transition liaison. Confirmed agenda this week includes general orientation, historical education, meeting with Congresswoman Taft (see attached schedule). Requests from Big Boy include access to Library of Congress (suggest remote access), acquisition of permanent wardrobe (suggest calling in on-site tailor services), visit to "authentic Filipino restaurant" (suggest take-out).

FOUR

THE VIEW FROM THE PENTHOUSE BALCONY was so bright it hurt Taft's eyes. Electric lights glittered across the city like a manmade firmament. Airplanes that must be the size of railcars roared overhead. He stood there gripping the handrail, the night air sighing across his bare and uncombed head, bringing with it the sounds of society and machinery he couldn't imagine. This, he knew, was only the beginning of the wonders this new century had to offer him.

The only wonder he wanted, though, was Nellie.

Taft had run the Philippines as governor-general, stood up to the robber barons at U.S. Steel, faced down hecklers on stages and train platforms from sea to shining sea. Along the way, people had called him a dullard; they'd called him a traitor to both the Republican Party and the progressive cause; they'd called him prejudiced. Every sharp word had cut him to the quick. And yet he'd weathered such storms with as much fortitude as he'd been able to muster while in the White House. Let them call him a bad president, a spineless one. It was better to have them think he was weak than to have them know the truth: that it was, more than anything else, an acute case of heartbreak that had all but assassinated the twenty-seventh president of the United States.

He remembered the day he'd first lost his wife. He'd been in office only two months; he and Nellie had been aboard the presidential yacht on a getaway to Mount Vernon. Nellie fainted. Ice was put to her temples and a brandy poured down her throat. By the time they'd made landfall, though, it was clear this was no bout of seasickness.

The stroke laid Nellie low, left her unable to speak. More than that, though, it was a cruel trick of fate that left a woman of such great life force infirm and isolated—a child learning to use her body again—just as she'd finally achieved her lifelong dream of becoming first lady.

She was still alive, and she fought hard to regain her faculties, thank the Lord for that. But the engine that drove Taft died that day in 1909, leaving him to finish out the rest of his long term just as hobbled as Nellie was. He'd downplayed it, of course, with his booming laugh and his beaming smile and his promises of national pride and equity. All that eroded quickly, of course. Taft was first deflated and then defeated.

And now, he'd lost Nellie a second time. A final time. He had nothing left. Washington, D.C., was laid out below him, but it may as well have been Bangkok.

"President Taft?" A woman's voice. Taft gripped the guardrail lest he launch himself over the thing.

"Ah, Miss Weschler." He spoke but didn't turn to face her. "You shouldn't sneak up on me so. I had quite forgotten you were on the premises." He felt a pang of guilt. The woman had been so kind to him, but, heavens, she needed to stop following him around like a little lost puppy.

"I, ah, I apologize. You were just so lost in thought out here, I was wondering if you might want to talk."

He snorted and wiggled his mustache. "Talk. That seems to be the major preoccupation of you people of the twenty-first century." He paused to let one of those violently loud mini-aircraft—what had Kowalczyk called it, a hell-copter? Appropriate name, given the infernal racket—shoot past overhead. "Ahem. Speaking of which. I started reading the notes you left me, Miss Weschler. On the twentieth century." He closed his eyes. "So, correct me if I'm wrong, madam: Scarcely five minutes after I left office, the entire world burst into war. Woodrow Wilson led America to victory. And then it happened again twenty years later, and Teddy Roosevelt's *cousin* led America to victory." Taft pressed the heels of his hands against his forehead. "The atom has been split. Men have traveled to the *Moon*. Only one president has been assassinated since McKinley—not bad, I suppose, statistically speaking. Palestine is a Jewish state and the Arabs would like it back. China is now the United States' largest debt-holder. China! And a singer named—what was it, Michael Jackman?—was the greatest artist of the twentieth century?"

"Well, that last one is open to debate."

"Indeed. It seems only yesterday the newspapers were falling over themselves to bestow the title upon that boy Al Jolson."

"Mr. Taft," she said quietly. "What do you think of all that? All those changes in the world?"

Finally, he turned to stare at her. "What would you have me say?"

"I don't mean to be pushy. It's just that . . . sometimes it feels better to talk. You know, about your feelings."

He snorted through his mustache. "I feel quite better shutting up, fine, thank you. In any case, I need to conserve my breath. Have you noticed how dreadful the air tastes? What do you people burn for fuel? Old shoes? In any case, besides an itch to play nine rounds at Chevy Chase and a tickle in my belly where my dinner isn't, I'm afraid I don't have any feelings to report."

She stepped forward and leaned against the rail next to him. "I mean your emotions."

He had to laugh at that. "Emotions? If you want emoting, Miss Weschler, I'll take you to a fine night at the theater."

It must have been the glare of the city—he could have sworn she blushed. "No, Mr. Taft, that's not what I meant exactly. I was just thinking you might be feeling scared. Or confused. Or maybe . . . alone."

"Oho!" Why hadn't he seen it coming? "I understand now, *Professor* Weschler. You have an ulterior motive here, don't you? You are a historian, are you not? Of the presidential persuasion? And picking my brain of its contents is surely a way for you to better your handicap among your peers, perhaps even secure a more auspicious post within the academy? Well, I won't be the butt of your ambition, Miss Weschler. I assure you, I'm not anybody's subject to be prodded, poked, and dissected. Since that first day in the White House, your doctors have gotten me medicated to the point that I'm sleepy and out of sorts half the day. I've had quite enough of that, I assure you, quite enough!"

He stormed back into the apartment and slammed the sliding glass door behind him.

A moment later, much more gently, he reopened it. "Oh, Miss Weschler, sorry to bother you. Just one more thing. Is there still a golf course nearby?"

From *Taft: A Tremendous Man*, by Susan Weschler:

I've been asked countless times: Why Taft? Why did I choose for my life's work to study this most hapless of one-term presidents? Was I just looking for an easy path to being the foremost expert in something, by picking a field that no one else cared about?

People are obsessed with greatness. Washington led the Revolution and founded the presidency. Lincoln brought us to victory over slavery and separatism. FDR reinvented the institutions of civic life with the New Deal. Kennedy stood up for civil rights and led us into space. Yes, these are all defining moments in our nation's history, in our human history. But the "great man" approach to history misses a much larger point: small moments also define us. In fact, aren't the small moments what *really* define us? It's the quiet little decisions we make every day that add up to who we are, from how we treat a homeless panhandler to whether we call our mothers and tell them we love them.

Taft didn't set out to leave his stamp on America, as Teddy Roosevelt did. But he understood that Roosevelt's crusade against corporate monopolies was a valiant one, and he kept on fighting the good fight, even after Teddy complained that he was doing it wrong.

Taft didn't win any wars. He also didn't start any. Interesting, isn't it, how the presidents with proper military experience are so often the ones most committed to maintaining peace?

Taft didn't champion any sweeping social legislation like the other politicians who called themselves progressives. But the laws that already existed? He never, ever, ever exempted himself from them. Never made the argument that the president gets to be special. Because he didn't think of himself as special. He thought of himself as an American—one among many.

We should all be such "great men."

Re: HERE'S WHAT I THINK ABOUT TAFT. (Foggy Bottom)

Date: 2011-11-15 9:42PM EST

I think Taft is the bomb diggity. I think Taft is dead fucking sexy. I think Taft ought to play Santa Claus in every mall in America. I think Taft would take down Chuck Norris in four seconds flat. I think Taft is one bad mutha (SHUT YO MOUTH). I think Taft is going to stick around for a while. I think Taft was long overdue.

Basically, I think Taft rocks my world. And really rocks that mustache. What do YOU think?

• Location: Foggy Bottom

"The first thing I noticed about my great-grandfather was his eyes. Well, no, I have to be honest, that was the second thing. The first thing I noticed was his size. Wow. You know, my whole family has a slight tendency toward being big boned—I've always been on the curvy side, and proudly so—but this was something else entirely. This wasn't healthy. All I could think was, you'd think that hibernating for a hundred years would have used up all that fat. But *then* I saw his eyes, and that made me forget about the other thing. The kindness, the pain, the empathy, the hopefulness—I just felt immediately at home with him. Here was my family. Any lingering doubts that I'd had vanished—not only about his identity, but about whether he'd deserved the sort of derision and scorn that had hounded him out of office and then kept hanging around his legacy after he disappeared. Meeting William Howard, I knew right away that, whether or not he was a great president, he was definitely an excellent man."

—*Congresswoman Rachel Taft,*
interview with NPR

FIVE

A T THIS MOMENT, Taft was sure he'd never felt so perfectly full. Not his belly—he wasn't even thinking about that. But his heart was full to bursting with warmth, even as his arms were full of the best hug he could remember.

He stepped back from the entryway of his apartment and held this woman at arm's length—this woman whose father's father had been his son Robert. He couldn't quite convince himself that he recognized his son in either her solid frame or her sturdy, kind features, but he also couldn't quite convince himself that he could speak without a lump forming in his throat.

Finally, she chuckled nervously. "I feel silly for asking, but—what should I call you?"

"Why," he said, wondrously, "I hadn't thought of that. I suppose Grandpa should do nicely."

At last he let her go and harrumphed deeply. "Would you like to sit down? Or, rather, I should say, I think I need to sit down." He motioned her toward the couch.

"Sorry, I'm a little overwhelmed, too." Rachel cleared her own throat, her eyes glittering. "Grandpa."

"So," he said. "I hear you've taken up the Taft banner and been tilting at windmills here in Washington."

"Oh, you have no idea. Or maybe you do." Taft nodded vigorously but said nothing; he'd picked up a bowl of candy from the coffee table and began rummaging through it, absent-mindedly popping pieces into his mouth, as she spoke. "It's business as usual, I guess. The Republicans won control of the House in the last midterms—that's when I was elected. The president's taking his cue from Clinton in '96 and hedging his agenda so that he can get some basic budget-balancing done. The polls aren't looking good for him, and the presidential election is only twelve months away. Primaries start soon. And the economy is still more or less a mess." She sighed. "At least we managed to avoid a second Great Depression."

"Second Great Depression? I'm assuming that means there was a first?"

"Um, yes. You just missed that back in your day. And the First World War."

"And the second one of those wasn't avoided." He gestured toward the computer on the desk in the corner of the room. "I've read a bit about them on this Internet of Susan's, but I've been a bit befuddled of late. And I type as if I have sausages instead of fingers."

Rachel smiled and suddenly stood. "Grandpa, I hate to reunite and run, but I'm due at the Capitol for a vote." She reached for her coat. "What are you doing for dinner, say, next Thursday?"

He blinked. "Next Thursday? I must say, I have no idea what I'll be doing tomorrow, let alone next Thursday."

"It's Thanksgiving," she said, walking to the door. "And I'll tell you exactly what you'll be doing: coming to Cincinnati to have Thanksgiving dinner with my family. With *your* family. I've already made the arrangements. You'll be flown out the day after tomorrow." She patted his belly. "You think you can save some room in there for turkey?"

Even beneath his mustache, Taft was fairly certain that the quiver in his lip as he pondered a holiday with family was visible. "Thanksgiving. Of course. That had quite slipped my mind. I . . . I'd like that very much, Rachel. I have a few pieces of correspondence to answer before then, but, yes, I think I'd quite like that."

"Then it's a deal, Mr. President." She hugged him, planted a quick kiss on his cheek, and shut the door behind her.

PAULINE CRAIG: With us today on *Raw Talk*: Jo L. Johnson, senior analyst at the Center for Right Ideas. Jo, talk to me about William Howard Taft, the Republican.

JO L. JOHNSON: Thank you, Pauline, it's good to be here. You know, Republicans usually remember President Taft, if at all, as something of a failure, a man who lost his reelection bid horribly—horribly!—to the Democrat Woodrow Wilson. Taft took only two states—it was a total embarrassment. But the thing is, when we look back at that 1912 election now from the right perspective, we realize that the only reason Taft lost is that Teddy Roosevelt decided he wanted to be president again, and when the Republican Party refused to kick Taft to the curb and welcome Roosevelt as their returning hero, he abandoned the GOP, started his own new third party, the Bull Moose Progressives, and jumped into the race anyway.

PAULINE CRAIG: So, basically, Roosevelt betrayed the sitting Republican president and the Republican Party and lost them the election. But because liberals write all the history books, Roosevelt still gets to be considered a hero for all time.

JO L. JOHNSON: That's right. If the conservative vote hadn't split, Taft might have won his second term. You know, he wasn't the sort of loud, crazy maverick that Roosevelt was.

PAULINE CRAIG: Well, today's Republican Party seems to have come to its senses after the last election and decided it's time to take a break from so-called progressive Republican mavericks and focus on good old-fashioned conservatives.

JO L. JOHNSON: That's right. There are definitely no RINOs hiding among the frontrunners right now—unless you count that former Massachusetts governor, but that's open to debate.

PAULINE CRAIG: A debate we'll save for another show. Now that Mr. Taft is back on the scene, what do you say: will he endorse one of the Republican candidates?

JO L. JOHNSON: Right now it's tricky to say for sure, but I would imagine that Mr. Taft will endorse one of them eventually. He was always a loyal Republican, and I'm sure once he has a chance to see the state of America today, he'll be eager to help put the party of common sense and American values back in charge.

PAULINE CRAIG: To right the ship of state, you might say.

JO L. JOHNSON: That's right.

SIX

MOMENTS AFTER WAKING, Taft was up and busy. He laid out the only suitable set of outdoor clothes his caretakers had given him. Curious things, they were: the fabrics were softer and flimsier than what he was used to, and, although they fit him passably, their cut was far more accommodating than he'd ever experienced. What really surprised him, though, was how little fashion appeared to have changed since his time—at least when it came to men. What women wore these days, he shuddered, was enough to send a man to a monastery. Or a cathouse.

Then he bathed, dressed, trimmed his mustache, made himself a quick snack of bacon and coffee and buttered toast, and prepared to convince his handlers that it was time to let him venture into the streets of Washington. Future or no, he wasn't doing anyone any good hiding in this damned apartment.

A knock came at the bedroom door. "Bill! It's me. I've got a little surprise for you. You decent?"

Taft hurried to pull on his pants. "I'll be right there, Kowalczyk!" He grabbed his coffee and marched out to the living room, where the agent was carrying a largish box under his arm.

"Bill, check this out," Kowalczyk said as he took off his jacket. He opened the box and began scattering its contents across the carpet.

"Wonderful," said Taft, mug in hand. "That looks like thirsty work. Would you like some coffee?"

"Not right now, thanks." He was wiring some kind of machine to the television set. Then, with a look of triumph on his face, he pulled out two white sticks from the box. "Look, Bill. You ready for a few holes?"

Taft stared. The white sticks looked like golf clubs. Kowalczyk laid them on the sofa and picked up a device Taft had learned was called a remote control—a miraculous time-saver, even though the loud, maddening chaos of the television gave him a headache if he watched it for more than ten minutes at a sitting.

Kowalczyk punched a couple buttons, and a picture was summoned to the screen. It was far from maddening. Just the opposite.

It was a golf course.

Taft almost dropped his coffee. "Well," he said under his breath, "what have we here."

Kowalczyk beamed at him. "Come on! Take a club. Give it a try." The agent didn't wait for him. He'd already moved the coffee table aside and readied himself to tee off. On the screen, an animated little man mimicked Kowalczyk's movements perfectly.

"Agent Kowalczyk," said Taft, with awe in his voice, "you golf?"

"No, Bill. *We* golf. Here."

Taft put down his mug and took the proffered club. It felt odd. Lightweight and crafted of plastic, its grip and heft were a far cry from a solid one-wood or three-iron. Still, the feel of the lance in his hand immediately calmed him. He remembered how much he'd been ridiculed in the press—hell, even by his own staff, party, and family—about his near-daily trips to the links. Golf, after all, was the leisure activity of the aristocrat. But it was his way of exercising, his way of clearing his head. And, most important, it was the line he drew between the demands of being the most powerful man in America and being simply an honest, plain fellow who needed green grass under his feet, fresh air in his lungs, and a blue sky overhead.

He assumed his address, aligned his club and body. Then he took a tentative test swing. The little man on the screen moved accordingly, like some kind of marionette connected to him by invisible strings. Taft couldn't help but giggle. "This is quite remarkable, Kowalczyk. Quite remarkable."

He readied himself again and then took a swing. He duffed.

"Damnation!" he howled in frustration. He tried again. This time, he took a deep breath and let his worries drain out of his head, down his spine, out his feet. True, there was no smell of shrubbery or tweeting of birds to lull him into a meditative state, as was often the case when he was on the course. But it was close enough; soon his breathing had slowed to a steady rhythm. Even his mind, which had been in such a half-drugged stupor over the past few weeks, had sharpened and focused on the shot at hand.

"Fore," he whispered. He let fly. The ball arced high into the air, above the trees. He watched it soar, the landscape whizzing by the ball on the screen as if by magic.

Then it landed. It bounced. It rolled.

Right into the cup.

"Bully! Kowalczyk, did you see that?" Taft thrust his half-club into the air. "Incredible. My first drive in a hundred years, and by golly it's a hole in one."

"Ready for the next one, Mr. President?"

Taft squared his body and stared into the magical glowing green. There'd be time to go outside after lunch. Or tomorrow.

http://www.etsy.com/listing/62899327/
clip-on-taft-mustache

HANDMADE! WILLIAM HOWARD TAFT
MUSTACHE

Did you know that William Howard Taft was the last president to wear a mustache? Now you can pay tribute with this stylish clip-on version. It's an absolute must-have accessory for any political junkie this season! You, too, can evoke the spirit of a more dignified American era at any costume party, activist rally, rock concert, or just for fun around town. Made of white felt flecked with silver glitter, it measures eight inches tip to tip. And it's styled just like Taft's signature crumb catcher, with both ends cheerily upturned so you can smile three times as hard as a wimpy clean-shaven person! Gentle plastic clip won't hurt your septum.

Ships from United States.

FROM THE DESK OF REP. RACHEL TAFT
(Ind.–OH)

Notes—Fri. 18th—meeting with Fulsom Foods lobbyist

—International Foods Act to include provisions governing proper handling of overseas livestock involved in producing food item imports. Fulsom lobbyist says impractical, will bankrupt small farmers. I point out Fulsom doesn't in fact work with small farmers but with poverty-wage laborers in giant agri-factories. Lobbyist suggests revisiting definition of "small farmers." I suggest Fulsom meditate on well-established definition of "regulation." Conversation is off to a great start.

—Is he serious? Fulsom wants to debate the definition of "food"? Not "processed food" or "raw food" or "organic food" or "healthy food," but the whole concept of food??? Is this to do with genetic modification? No—what he calls "more sophisticated" method of chemical synthesis. Will look at their white paper but am highly dubious to say least.

—No, I cannot give out a mailing address at which Wm Howard might receive housewarming gift of a Fulsom Baskotti Bounty. Come on, now.

CLASSIFIED
Secret Service Incidence Report
BBO20111119.005
Agent Ira Kowalczyk

At 0925, guard detail attempted to escort Big Boy to visit Library of Congress on foot, per his insistence. Made it two blocks east before rock-star phenomena kicked in: crowd amassed at a faster rate than the expedition's walking speed. Big Boy was swarmed by civilians. Guard maintained tight perimeter, but the crowd was too enthusiastic to maintain a respectful distance per my instructions. Mob stopped short of being a riot, with everyone smiling and cheering and waving and snapping cell-phone photos, but the expedition was obviously unsustainable in this fashion so we returned to Big Boy One. Big Boy insists on going out again despite the security risk, so we will try it incognito. He won't shave off his mustache, so we'll trim it as small as he'll let us and put him in a T-shirt and baseball cap.

SEVEN

I F IT WEREN'T FOR THE STREET SIGNS, Taft would have already been lost. Even in his own day, the city had been a labyrinth, at least compared to Cincinnati. Granted, Cincinnati was a far larger city. But Cincinnati had been a *home*. A genial city, an honest city. Washington, however, was run by a perverse logic as confounding as the city's layout. Taft's mind, sharp as it was, had always knotted itself into a pretzel trying to figure it out, just as his calves knotted now as he ambled in the general direction of Union Station and the Supreme Court.

"What I wouldn't give for a stiff rubdown with some witch hazel," he muttered, smiling as he did so at an elderly woman passing him on the sidewalk. She scowled at him as if he he'd wagged his tongue at her. "And that's another difference between Washington and Cincinnati," he added as soon as she was out of earshot.

Oh, but it felt good to stretch his legs and see people, no matter how surly they might be, no matter what ridiculous clothes he had to wear or how many plainclothes agents were in a ten-foot radius. His head felt clearer than it had in a long, long time. Even before his hibernation—he snorted at the word's ursine connotation; surely some venomous journalist had already applied it to him—things had been tumultuous. The election had been a disastrous affair all around, a humiliation inexorably unfolding around him day by day for a solid half-year as Teddy—his friend, his mentor, the very man who'd encouraged him to run for president in the first place—stepped back into the limelight to denigrate Taft's performance with ever more colorful language, ever more vehement invective.

And yet, the electorate had loved that about Teddy, hadn't they? They loved his safari-hunting, warmongering, hot-air-spouting passion. By the time November rolled around, even Taft had been resigned to the situation. Wilson seemed a solid enough fellow. Let *him* spend every night losing sleep over the world's endless, bloody conflicts! And, in all honesty, Taft had felt a massive weight leave his shoulders the instant Wilson and his wife stepped into the White House that morning in March of 1913. Already Taft had been looking forward to returning to Cincinnati, finding work, perhaps even going on a real diet. He'd tried to manage his weight while in office, but then, out of the limelight, he hoped to peel off the extraneous seventy pounds he'd put on since being sworn in four years prior.

Of course, he'd never had the chance. As he rounded a corner onto D Street, he tried to focus his newly sharpened thoughts on the day he'd disappeared. All he could remember was taking a walk in the rain—then waking up with Butt chasing him across the South Lawn—

Wait. Butt? He'd meant Kowalczyk, of course. How odd.

Then it all came back to him. Butt. His aide-de-camp. His dearest friend. He had died—but not *after* Taft's disappearance. Butt had died in April 1912, along with his traveling companion on the *Titanic*, Francis Millet. That's why Taft had built the Millet-

Butt Memorial Fountain, just across the way from the South Lawn
Fountain. That's why Taft had, in his oafishness, blundered toward
the fountains after waking. It was one of the few things his exhumed
brain had been able to remember.

Taft shuddered. It was only just past noon, but a chill had crept
into his bones. He pulled his coat tighter about him. His stomach
grumbled.

"I hear you, old friend," he said, changing course abruptly and
crossing the street, incurring the wrath of a honking and altogether
too fast automobile. So much was new in Washington; a hundred
years, after all, was a hundred years. But surely there were some
things from the old days that remained. "Yes, I hear you."

THE COUNTER OF WALDEMANN'S DELI hadn't changed.
Taft had to restrain himself from rubbing his eyes. The televisions
in the corners of the room never used to be there, of course. And
people surely never used to sit at the tables while speaking on their
telephones. These telephones—so tiny, and no cables!—should have
surprised Taft, but oddly they did not. In fact, he was more surprised
when Susan had told him wireless telephones had come into vogue
only a few years earlier. In his time, Marconi's telegraphy had
successfully transmitted Morse code between ships on open water.
For some reason, he'd assumed they'd all have wireless telephones
in his own lifetime.

That was to say, his natural lifetime.

But the rest of it looked the same. The gleaming counters.
The checkered-tile floors. Even—yes!—the framed photograph
of Taft and Butt hanging on the wall, although it had faded and
collected dust to the point of being almost unrecognizable. He
started to call Kowalczyk in from the door, where he stood guard,
to show him the memento, before he remembered that incognito

was the order of the day.

"You gonna order?" The gruff voice came from behind the counter, but all Taft could see was the top of a bald head with a paper hat perched askew there on it.

Taft froze. That voice. He knew it.

"Mr. Waldemann?"

The short man peered up at him from behind the counter. He wielded a cleaver in one hand and a bottle of mustard in the other. "No, it's the Meat Fairy. Come on, I ain't got all day. What's your order?"

Taft couldn't believe it. Surely Mr. Waldemann, the proprietor of Waldemann's Deli, had been dead for decades. Yet here stood his spitting image.

Of course. Waldemann's had always been a family business. Three generations of Waldemanns had worked behind the same counter together when Taft and Butt had come here every Thursday for lunch. It was one of their rituals; each week, under the pretext of a round of golf, the two of them would sneak out, evade the Secret Service, and stroll down to Waldemann's for a brisket sandwich. He felt for all the world like a boy playing hooky again; he and Butt would laugh and gossip about the White House staff while gorging themselves on sandwiches as tall and as wide as their hats.

And this little man? Why, he must be Waldemann's descendent. His voice, his temperament, his lack of height: all Waldemann.

"Yes, sir. My apologies. I'd like a double brisket sandwich on rye, if you please. And an egg cream."

"On rye, eh? As opposed to . . . ?" He lowered his head, grumbled, and began slapping at the side of an electric meat-shaving contraption. Once the rickety machine reached a sufficiently high pitch, he began feeding a skull-sized chunk of beef into it.

The smell engulfed Taft. Oh, how he'd loved these sandwiches.

He'd always had a hard time explaining just how comforted food made him feel. When the world was at his door and the dogs were barking at his heels, eating was the best way to take his mind off it all. The orderliness with which he ate his food, the fastidious way he'd mop up each morsel. . . . He knew that, in many ways, he spent so much time eating simply as a means of procrastination. He'd always had that problem, even as an athletic and relatively well built young man. But what was one to do when facing the enormity of all the world's problems? Especially when, without fail, they all wound up on his desk?

"Order up!" yelled Waldemann, who then rang a bell on the counter. The same bell the Waldemanns had always rung. The sound made Taft's mouth burst into salivation. At the end of the counter sat a monumental sandwich and what may well have been a half-gallon of egg cream in a tall, frosty glass.

Taft had to keep himself from running to the cash register. Once there, he pulled out the wallet Kowalczyk had given him. "Here, good sir. How much will it be?"

"Nine seventy-five."

Taft gaped. He looked at the cash register to make sure he'd heard right. A sawbuck? For a lone man's lunch? What had *happened* to this country? He'd have to look into the state of the economy. As soon, of course, as he'd finished this marvelous-looking sandwich. As Waldemann stared at him, Taft flipped through the wallet's contents, pulling out and then pocketing a series of what appeared to be colorful, rigid business cards. Finally he found the (odd-looking!) currency. He handed a $10 bill to Waldemann, who squinted at him.

"Keep the change, dear fellow." Taft grinned at his own munificence.

"A whole quarter? Gee, you're too kind."

Indeed, Taft had to agree.

Duly equipped with sustenance, Taft found the table toward the back of the small eatery, the one that had been unofficially reserved for him and Butt during the era of their frequent patronage. Remarkably—and, he liked to muse, due to his unassuming nature—he seemed to go mostly unrecognized during their weekly lunches. But at least once a month, a wide-eyed patron would approach him and either ask to shake his hand or make some unceremonious quip about the girth of both his gut and his government.

But that was before. Today, a woman sat at his table, buried in a newspaper, oblivious to his presence.

"Excuse me, ma'am," he said, approaching from across the table. "I would like to ask you a favor. This table has . . . a certain sentimental attachment to me. Would you at all mind if I asked you to move?"

The woman peered over the top of her paper at him. She was middle aged and a light-skinned Negro, Taft now noticed—no, he must remember to think *African American,* as Miss Weschler had told him was now proper—but dressed deceptively young for her age. She blew across her cup of coffee, her eyes still on him. "You know, it's been fifty years since a white man made me give him my seat. I'm not so sure I want to go back to that right now."

Taft didn't quite catch the meaning of her words, but he got the cut of her jib.

"My deepest apologies, ma'am. I didn't mean to put you out."

"I was joking. No offense taken." She smiled. "I'll tell you what. I'm not in the mood to move to another table, but you're more than welcome to join me."

Taft grinned and sat down. "My name is Bill," he offered.

"Well, of course it is, dear. My name is Dee Dee." She held out her hand.

What a remarkably self-possessed woman! "Delighted," he said, taking it. Bold and strong—now that's how one shakes hands, regardless of one's gender. His mother had shaken hands that way. Nellie, too.

"Out for a stroll, Bill?"

"Yes, indeed! I've always loved a brisk day in D.C. Sometimes it's the only thing that can lift my spirits."

She nodded toward the sandwich he'd already begun attacking. "That and some brisket."

"Too true, too true. You know, Dee Dee," he said, washing down a mouthful of meat with a swallow of rich, sweet egg cream, "D.C. isn't my native land, but I do believe that if I'd ever lived here by choice rather than necessity, I'd have come to enjoy it much more than I do."

"I hear that. I'm no native either. I'm from New Orleans. Katrina made me move up here, to live with my daughter."

"And who is this interloping Katrina?" he asked, abandoning the egg cream's inadequate straw and tipping back the glass for a gulp.

She laughed. "Oh, you are too funny. Here." She picked up a napkin and reached toward his face. "You've got that stuff all over your mustache."

Taft didn't flinch. What a novel development. Clearly, a white man and a Negro woman sitting together in a restaurant was of no matter in the twenty-first century. He was less surprised than perhaps he should have been. He was, after all, a Republican, a member of the party of progress. In his heart of hearts, he had always believed it an inevitability that racial tensions would somehow ease as America grew and prospered, and that "separate but equal" was but a temporary measure.

Some had thought the president should address the question. But for the executive branch to overstep its boundaries and poke its nose into such social matters was, in Taft's estimation, unconstitutional. Of course . . . he hadn't balked at stretching executive power to bust trusts or form the Postal Savings System. Was he merely rationalizing his handling of the Negro issue? Had he been a coward? If so, it wouldn't be the first time he'd shied away—or outright *run* away—from one of the many urgent issues that had pressed like the stone of Sisyphus upon his administration.

"There," said Dee Dee, wiping the last of the egg cream from his whiskers, "that's better. Lord, are you always such a mess?"

"Just a hearty eater," he said with a chuckle. "Some say I'm famous for it."

"Oh, really?" She leaned across the table, a mischievous look on her face. "Bill, I'll let you in on a little secret. I know who you are."

"Oh?"

"Uh-huh. Seen you on TV. You were even in my history books when I was a little girl."

Taft felt a blush creep up his neck. "History books. I must confess, that's rather flattering."

"Flattering? Bill, you're legendary! The Great Missing President. The man with the mustache. The bathtub guy."

Taft's face drooped. "Bathtub? People still talk about that?" He pushed away his plate, which he realized he'd emptied without knowing it. "What else do you know about me? What else do the history books say?"

"Oh, don't fret. People don't pay much attention to history anymore." She glanced past Taft, and her eyes narrowed. "Except for Waldemann over there. Bill . . . is that your fan club?"

Taft looked over his shoulder. Waldemann had approached the Secret Service agents and appeared to be suspiciously interrogating them. In his hand, the deli owner held the framed photo of Taft and Butt that had been on the wall, presumably undisturbed, for over a hundred years. A rectangle of brighter paint marked the spot where it had hung.

With his other hand, Waldemann was pointing at him.

Dee Dee nudged Taft's glass of egg cream. "I think you've been made, Bill. Better drink up." She stood up and gathered her coat and purse. He could have sworn she winked at him. "Sorry our little chat had to get cut short. Maybe I'll run into you for lunch some day. If they ever let you out again."

KCMO Talk Radio 710

The following message is paid for by Kansas City Leaders for Responsible Development.

Three years into the worst American economy since the Great Depression, we don't need government inventing more and more taxes to weigh down hardworking small-business owners. But the elitists on the Kansas City Council just don't understand. *They* think you can afford to pay higher taxes every year, even though you're making less. The small-business tax rate this year is already as high as *39 percent*. It's enough to make you wish for the days of William Howard Taft. After all, when Taft was president, businesses paid only *1* percent. Tell you what, City Council—next year, why don't you try thinking a little more like Taft?

From Taft: *A Tremendous Man*, by Susan Weschler:

During the course of America's existence every type of man has been president: schemers, brutes, drunkards, braggarts—even a few good men. But there was one thing they all shared: the burning ambition to be president.

But not Taft. Of all the U.S. presidents who followed George Washington, only Taft never aspired to the office. He'd always felt his true calling was on the Supreme Court, an honor he was painfully forced to bestow on others while he served as president. Afterward, he'd retreat to his own office and count the minutes until his four-year term was up. Some historians wondered: Was it selfish to be a reluctant president? Shouldn't he have resigned if he'd hated it so much? In a word: no. Because Taft had people depending on him, and no matter what he might wish for himself, he would never let them down. People like his wife, Nellie, and his friend Roosevelt, both of whom did have selfish motives for pushing and pulling Taft into office. Nellie had always dreamed of being first lady, and Roosevelt wanted a successor who'd honor him, who'd continue his policies without ever outshining him.

Power corrupts, goes the aphorism. But Taft tasted power—tremendous power—and instead of being seduced by it, he was repulsed by it.

What kind of character does such a man possess? This question consumed me when I began studying history in earnest. And the more I learned about him, the more I wished I'd had the chance to meet this man. Just once. Just to say, *The country may not have appreciated you. History may not have vindicated you. And since you disappeared on your first day as a free man, you never had the chance to prove them wrong, to find your true calling, to find happiness. But I understand you. I admire you. I know how you feel—because I feel the same way.*

And then, of course, the impossible happened, and I did meet him. His portraits didn't do him justice. Sturdy, solid, protective without being patronizing, manly without being boorish. And with that distinguished mustache—the last mustache a U.S. president would ever wear. I sometimes suspect Taft was the reason later presidents stopped wearing facial hair. Anything to set themselves apart from the president who had become a cipher at best, a punch line at worst.

If they only knew.

FROM THE DESK OF REP. RACHEL TAFT (Ind.–OH)

To-do list—Tues. 22nd—Things to discuss with Grandpa

—Won't do any political appearances while we're home. But maybe we can take just one picture with the Cincinnati Little League?

—Thanksgiving dinner. Please invite Agent Kowalczyk to join us at the table.

—Please remember next time someone recognizes you that we all have cameras in our phones now. Phone waving is not a ritual greeting.

—Gay people. General catching up about all that.

—Your great-great-granddaughter is biracial. Please please oh god please don't be weird about it. If you are, we'll all deal. But please don't. Oh hell.

EIGHT

FIRST IT HAD BEEN THE YOUNG MAN behind the bar at the airport restaurant. Now a whole crowd, albeit a small one, had gathered around Taft. Some were old. Some were young. Some were black. Some were white. Some had accents. Others didn't. But they all had one thing in common: they wanted his autograph.

Apparently his twenty-first-century informal look only went so far.

"Yes, you there, my good fellow. Pass that newspaper over, and I'll give it a good endorsing." Rachel, bless her heart, had tried to keep them away at first, ordering Kowalczyk and his six-man Secret Service detail to form a barrier around Taft and walk him straight to the gate where his airplane was boarding. At first, that seemed sensible. But as the trickle of hangers-on became a small but swift current, he remembered his promise to Rachel. No more hiding out. No more running away.

He wished Susan hadn't chosen to stay behind. The thought of her alone for Thanksgiving made his stomach somersault. As did the thought of the holiday itself. He had no idea what Thanksgiving dinners were like in this day and age, but he hoped that a big, fresh, juicy turkey remained the tradition. Hell, he'd eat Twinkies in place of pumpkin pie if he could just have a sizeable platter of gravy-drenched turkey.

"There you go, little girl. And you, ma'am, what would you like me to sign?" An alarmingly comely young woman pulled down the collar of her blouse—exceedingly thin and skimpy, as seemed to be the fashion in this shameless new century—as if to indicate her bosom.

"Ah, thank you, no. Might you have a piece of paper?" He signed an envelope she was holding and moved on to the next person, walking slowly along as he did.

The next person—a young man with a particularly puckish look on his face—offered Taft a small, flat, shiny box to sign. Upon it were the words *President Kane*. Before he could get a good look at it, Kowlaczyk snatched it out of the man's hand and had one of the other agents hustle him away.

"What was that?"

Kowalczyk traded glances with Rachel. Was that a grimace of conspiracy on their faces? No, it couldn't be. He was being, as Nellie used to say, far too sensitive.

"Just a DVD, sir. A movie. Nothing you need to be bothered with."

"A moving picture? In a little box? Why, that sounds exactly like something I need to be bothered with."

Rachel put her face near his ear. "Are you doing okay?" she whispered. If Taft didn't know better, he'd say she was changing the subject. "Really, I'd have no problem with Kowalczyk moving these people back. They're like vultures."

He laughed. "And when has the public ever not? Besides, I'm honestly a bit terrified about this traveling through the air business."

"It'll be fine. We just need to get to the damn plane already. At least it's a private jet. If we were flying commercial, we'd be screwed right about now."

Taft moved on to the next outstretched piece of paper in his path. "All I know is this: if Teddy Roosevelt could go up in an airplane, so can I." He remembered that day in October 1910 when he was sitting in the Oval Office and got the telephone call from Teddy. "Bill! You'll never believe what I did today. The Wright Brothers themselves gave me a ride in one of their biplanes! Glorious! You should see what the earth looks like from such a height. The reporters are on their way now. I just wanted to share this magnificent moment with you."

That was Teddy. He always had to look down on you. It had become obvious to Taft, mere weeks after his election in 1908, that Roosevelt already chafed at seeing someone else in *his* White House. Even as a civilian, he had to blow his horn louder and make a bigger spectacle than the president himself. It was a petulant way to draw attention, but hadn't that always been Teddy's way? Taft was steady, deliberate, grounded. Teddy climbed into winged contraptions and laughed as they hurtled through the sky. It was hard for Taft to believe that it wasn't all part of Teddy's plan—to undermine Taft's presidency, to constantly remind the American people that, mere months earlier, they'd had a virile and heroic commander-in-chief. Oh, and trim, too.

Was he still dwelling on the election? Curse it all. A hundred years had slipped by. He'd have to learn to get over it.

Suddenly Taft realized his procession had slowed from a crawl to a halt. What was it now? Blast it. Thinking of Teddy always had a way of stirring up his nerves.

"Mr. President. May I have a word with you? It's about our correspondence."

A woman, perhaps in early middle age, stood before him. She wore a cap and glasses tinted so dark he couldn't see her eyes.

"Excuse me? I'm sorry, ma'am, but I'm quite sure I've not made your acquaintance."

She stepped forward, bumped against the formidable barricade of Kowalczyk's outstretched arm, and lowered her glasses to the tip of her nose. "President Taft, it's me. Pauline Craig. From TV."

And so it was. Even behind the glasses and beneath the ridiculous hat, she was striking. Hard-faced, composed, controlled, with an almost chiseled beauty—in person she reminded Taft uncannily of Nellie.

"Ah, why, yes, Mrs. Craig—"

"Ms. Craig."

"Yes, Ms. Craig. How caddish of me. Did you receive my reply to your invitation? I had so many missives to answer this week before preparing for the holiday."

"I did. And that's what I'm here to talk to you about." She shifted her bag under her arm. "Can you spare a moment?"

"No, he can't." It was Kowalczyk. Taft suddenly hated his new friend with a passion. "Get your autograph or move along, please."

"I just wanted to ask you, Mr. Taft, why you refuse to appear on my show. Your reply didn't give much of an explanation."

Taft bristled. "Look here, madam. I used to get in far too much trouble by accepting invitations from every muckraker who happened along. I do sincerely appreciate your invitation, and perhaps in the future—"

"Mr. Taft," she said, taking off her glasses. Her icy blue eyes lanced him to the quick. "It *is* the future. And the future needs you. You can't dodge your destiny, sir."

"And what destiny would that be?"

"Politics, of course. You're advising your great-granddaughter, aren't you? What are you planning? Is there a new dynasty in the making here? Taft 2012, perhaps? The public has a right to know, Mr. Taft!"

At that point, Kowalczyk had had enough. "Okay, lady, you've had your chat, and we have a plane to catch."

The agent's coterie fell into phalanx formation and pointed Taft on down the walkway. Pauline Craig was swept away in a swarm of bodies and chaos, but not before yelling, "Taft 2012! Is that what this is all about? Mr. Taft! Congresswoman! The nation is waiting for answers!"

Her voice trailed off as the Secret Service herded them in opposite directions. Again, the void in Taft's gut felt as though it threatened to consume him. Again, his life was quickly spiraling out of his control.

CLASSIFIED
Secret Service Incidence Report
BBO20111124.015
Agent Ira Kowalczyk

At 1059, touched down at Cincinnati. Advance team confirms Grand Girl's residence and Big Boy's requested detour to Patterson both secure. No crowds in the airport on this end; possibly it's just the D.C. populace that's grown inured to the incognito approach.

===================

cincinnati craigslist > personals > missed connections

Re: DID WM HOWARD TAFT TRIM HIS STACHE?
(Airport)
Date: 2011-11-24 11:36 AM EST
     Because I think I just saw him in Concourse B.
     I didn't want to bother the guy, though—it's a holiday.
• Location: Airport

NINE

CINCINNATI WASN'T anything like he remembered. And it was exactly like he remembered.

What differed was the skyline. The buildings—so many more of them!—seemed like sad hulks pitted against the cosmos, crumbling guardians infested from within and taken for granted by their wards. In his day, Cincinnati was a city on its way up. New architecture, new commerce, new industry. It was clear, without having to consult any history book, that things had changed.

At the same time, the encroaching winter smelled and felt the same in his lungs and on his skin as it ever did. Rolling down the window of the automobile that carried them from the airport, he savored that familiar bouquet of frost and steam and industry, although, he had to admit, the air seemed cleaner than it had in his day. It stung his nose, but, more than that, it stung his memory.

"Rachel!" he said suddenly, rummaging around in one of his bags. "I'd completely forgotten. I know you must be in a rush to get home to your husband, as I am to meet him. But is there a chance we might make a stop along the way?" He produced an opened envelope from his luggage and handed it to her. "Can you please pass this up to the driver? The address is on it."

"What is this?" she said, turning it over.

"Just an almost acquaintance, one whose actual making is long overdue."

Rachel, thankfully, didn't pester or question him the way Susan would have. She nodded and spoke to the driver, who pulled the car off the busy thoroughfare and was soon cutting through a series of slushy side streets. It had started snowing, and a light dusting of tiny flakes drifted through the air like angels.

Within minutes, they'd arrived. Taft asked for the envelope back from the driver, and he double-checked the address with the one on the building. This was it. Patterson Senior Village.

"Kowalczyk, do you mind waiting?" he said as he opened the door and stepped into the snow. "I assure you, there's no one of dangerous intent in there."

"I know," the agent said. "I'll come into the building anyway. But don't worry, I'll leave you to your private conversation. Oh, that reminds me—" He handed Taft one of those small, miraculous telephones everyone seemed to have permanently attached to their ears. "My number's on speed dial. Here, let me show you. Just hit the number one if you ever need to call me, two for Susan, and three for Rachel. Sound good?"

Taft held the tiny device in his hand then slipped it into the pocket of his overcoat. It was thoughtful of Kowalczyk, but he certainly wouldn't be needing it here. This telephone was a marvel of the future. He was here to speak to the past.

THE HALLS SMELLED like some sort of sickening mixture of medicine and candy. Come to think of it, the walls also imagined the color of such a mingling. Taft had had no problem getting past the front desk; he knew he'd already been added to the list of potential visitors, a fat, hopeful clipboard full of unchecked names that the clerk at the desk had referenced before calling an orderly to escort him to the room.

He passed open doorways that added a mild tang of urine and disinfectant to the already cloying odor. Taft felt a twinge somewhere in his midsection and wished suddenly that he hadn't been nauseous on the aircraft.

Finally, they arrived at the door: Room 128. As the orderly knocked, announced the visitor, and turned the doorknob, Taft wondered at the notion of having one's environment, one's entire existence, reduced and restricted to one building, one room. He realized sadly that, during his time in office, he'd known that feeling all too well.

The door swung open. The air, thankfully, become sweeter, bearing a heady bouquet of rosewater. "Well, are you gonna stand out there all day?" The voice was ragged around the edges, but the woman to whom it belonged couldn't have looked less so.

Ms. Irene O'Malley—or rather, Irene Kaye, as the widow had retained her long-departed husband's last name—sat on the edge of the bed, all 100 pounds and 105 years of her. A quilt fit for a bee lay in a state of construction across her lap. Her long, silver hair was done up in a simple braid. In her bony fingers flashed a needle. She didn't stop stitching or even glance up as Taft walked into the room. The orderly left the two alone.

"Sit down, please," said Irene, indicating a chair next to her bed piled high with newspapers. Taft picked up the heavy stack and grunted as he placed it on the floor next to an even larger stack.

"I never had much use for the newspapers while I was in office," he grumbled as he eased his bulk into the seat. He looked at Irene, whose eyes sparkled deeply in their nests of pink wrinkles.

Still, her skin almost glowed. She seemed preternaturally hale, healthy, and alert for one so old. Taft wondered briefly at the status of medicine in America. These days, it must be a veritable marvel of equity and efficiency.

"Thank you for writing me, Mrs. Kaye," he began.

"Oh, call me Irene," she said. "Just Irene. That's who I was the first time I wrote to you. When I was six."

"I wish I had answered you at the time," Taft said. "What good is a president if he can't take the time out to reply to a child, to help inspire the future?"

Irene shrugged extravagantly. "Well, the future is here. I survived regardless. And I must say, you now look young enough to be my grandson."

"What has your life been like, Irene? That is, if you don't mind my asking. These people who are watching over me now, they . . . they don't understand. They weren't alive back then. It seems like such a different world in so many ways. How did you make it to the twenty-first century without going mad?"

"Well, I suppose I did it the same way you made it from the nineteenth to the twentieth. It was gradual. You go along with things. And when you can't, you let things flow on past you and try not to obstruct them."

"That's a sensible way of looking at it."

"Sensibility may be the only good quality I have left." She chuckled. "Half my eyesight is gone. My youngest son passed away over ten years ago. I still have my mind, though. And my memories."

"Tell me of them, please. What was the rest of the twentieth century like? What have I missed?"

She seemed taken aback. "Haven't your government people been telling you?"

He sighed. "Even if they were my age, they should be a century too young to offer the perspective I need."

"Well," said Irene, "I'd be happy to tell you what I know. But it would take a while, and you have friends waiting."

"I know the perfect solution. Irene, would you like to have Thanksgiving dinner with me and my family? I could have a car sent tomorrow."

"Oh, I couldn't impose. There's also this small matter." She lifted her arm, displaying a tangled trail of tubes that led from a machine next to her bed and into her body. "They've got me all trussed up here. But I tell you what: If you happen to have any leftovers you'd like to bring me, I'd be happy to take care of them for you."

He took her hand. "Of course. But only if you promise me that you'll tell me more about yourself. I thirst for conversation with someone who remembers ragtime and Bob Bescher and the day the *Titanic* didn't come home."

"Bob Bescher! Now there's a name I haven't heard in ages."

He laughed. "How are the Reds doing in this day and age, by the by?"

"Oh, dear. You don't want to know."

Taft looked away, lost abruptly in thought. "Baseball! I know, in the grand scheme of things, it's a trivial pastime. But for some reason the notion that baseball is still an institution in this nation . . . it makes me think things haven't changed all that much, despite everything I've learned to the contrary." He put down her hand and picked up his hat and coat. "Did you know, Irene, that I'm the only president to have ever thrown the first pitch of the baseball season? In 1910, Senators versus Athletics. It was a big to-do! And my pitching arm isn't half bad, if I do say so myself. Ah, what a grand day."

She smiled. "Pretty much every president since you has done

the same thing." Then she saw the look on his face and patted his hand. "But you were the first."

The warmth of Irene's room and words and presence carried him out the door and through the cold and back to the car where Rachel and Kowalczyk waited. His brain swirled with nebulous questions and memories he couldn't capture long enough to name.

Fox News Poll

Do you think America is stronger today than it was 100 years ago?

Yes: 28 percent
No: 72 percent

========================

Channel 12 Cincinnati News Poll

Do you approve of the job Rep. Rachel Taft (Ind.) is doing in Congress?

(October 23)
Yes: 41 percent
No: 47 percent
Undecided: 12 percent

(November 23)
Yes: 54 percent
No: 43 percent
Undecided: 3 percent

TEN

THE SNOW WAS FALLING at full speed—a great, fat, wet Cincinnati snow—by the time the car arrived at Rachel's house. For some reason, this sudden onset of winter energized him. As Taft stomped his shoes on Rachel's front step, he almost regretted having to enter the bright warmth that radiated from her open door.

That same warmth, however, wasn't coming from Rachel. She'd grown increasingly terse and withdrawn as the blocks melted away and the car drew closer to her home. Taft didn't know why and didn't dare ask. He was the last person to pass judgment on the tempest of another's soul, so long as that tempest harmed no one. But he swore, as she led him through the door of her house, that Rachel would rather she were inviting the Abominable Snowman to eat Thanksgiving dinner with her family. Or to *eat* her family.

"Um, please take off your shoes, Grandpa," she mumbled absently as she closed the door behind them. "You can leave them here."

Take off his shoes? Was this some religious observance? He

shrugged and followed her lead, then hung his coat and hat on a hook on the wall nearby. Meanwhile Rachel seemed to be steadying herself for something—like, say, an oncoming train.

"Are you all right? You seem a little . . . out of sorts."

She smiled a weak smile. "Sorry. It's just that . . . Oh, never mind. Let's just get this over with. Trevor! Trevor, honey, we're home."

"Coming!" Taft had to admit he liked his great-grandson-in-law already, from his voice alone. Strong, deep of timbre, full of character. Rachel had told him briefly that her husband was a lawyer, but she didn't dwell on it, and she'd shown him no photos. No matter. Here he came around the corner, tall and broad shouldered and beaming and . . .

And black.

Taft stared. He could almost feel the air curdle around Rachel, who stood next to him, wound as tightly as a spring. This was why she'd been vague about her husband. She'd married a . . . an African American. Things had changed since 1913, and for the better. The sitting president was black. But this . . . He didn't know what to think. Mixed marriages had not been unknown in his own time, of course. And he was in favor of them, though polite conversation would rarely edge toward such a subject. But his own family. He knew what he *should* feel: nothing but happiness for Rachel. But as this emotion flashed through his mind in that split second, so did another, less charitable one. Taft wasn't proud of it. But there it was, as bitter and nasty as a clove of garlic dropped in a sauce.

Trevor must have seen the apprehension in Taft's eyes, and in Rachel's. Just as he rounded the corner, he halted, a smile frozen on his face. It began to harden. The air was thick with a tension that made Taft's arm hair stand on end.

A second passed. Then another excruciating, interminable second. A bead of sweat trickled down Taft's face.

Someone say something, his mind screamed.

"Grandpa!"

All of a sudden, a child's voice broke the silence like a hammer through museum glass. From behind Trevor's legs came a little girl, her skin almost as dark as his, her hair in beaded rows and a doll in her hand.

Not just any doll. As the girl ran to him, Taft saw it was a miniature, stuffed-toy version of *him*, complete with a puffy belly and a fuzzy mustache.

He looked at Trevor. He looked at Rachel. He looked at the girl. What could he do? As she ran toward him, he bent down and scooped her up. Her tiny limbs flailed against his great girth. As he picked her up, she hugged him.

It was quite possibly the most wonderful thing he'd felt in his life.

TAFT SAT BACK from the dinner table. He was perfectly content, and the turkey couldn't take full credit. Granted, it wasn't exactly a turkey they'd eaten that night; as Rachel and Trevor had described it, the delicious meat they'd devoured along with their mashed potatoes and gravy and yams wasn't a whole turkey at all, but an Fulsom TurkEase, a last-minute replacement they'd been forced to buy after the local grocery had run out of real birds.

"Really, Grandpa, we try not to eat so much processed junk," Rachel explained as she passed the cranberries. "But sometimes, in a pinch, what else can you do?"

Abby—all three and a half feet and six years of her—piped up. "They showed us a video in school. They make this stuff with smushed turkey. The bones and everything. They make pink toothpaste out of turkey and then color it with turkey color."

Taft looked at the forkful that hovered a mere inch from his open mouth. "Oh, really? That's quite an imagination you have, little one! Back in my day, President Theodore Roosevelt passed the Pure Food and Drug Act. Things like that aren't allowed to make it to market."

Rachel glanced at Trevor and laughed.

"Did I say something funny?"

"No, Grandpa. It's just that . . . things aren't quite as clear-cut. As much as I hate to admit it, food-industry lobbyists spend millions every year making sure companies like Fulsom get to do whatever they want. I'm working on passing a bill right now that—"

"Oh no, Rachel." Taft grinned and shoveled more of the succulent future-turkey into his mouth. "We'll not talk politics over the Thanksgiving dinner table. Things can't be that bad! After all, here we all are eating this wonderful meal. Let's find something else to discuss." He winked at Abby. "For instance, what this young lady might want for Christmas."

Abby's smile showed a missing tooth that only made her that much more adorable. At first he didn't see it, but now it was evident: she was a Taft all right, from her eyes to the set of her forehead. He looked at Trevor and Rachel, and pride practically oozed from his pores.

"I'd like another Grandpa doll, please. A bigger one, so I can bring it to show-and-tell."

"Why settle for a homunculus when you have the real thing?" He thumped his chest. "Bring me to class. I'll be your show-and-tell."

That set Abby off into gales of giggles. When she calmed down, she excused herself and wandered into the next room. Next to her empty seat sat Kowalczyk, eating with his head down, as if looking at no one might somehow render him invisible.

"Kowalczyk, my good man! How goes your meal? You've hardly said a word since you got here. Is everything well?"

Kowalczyk nodded tersely and kept eating.

Then it struck Taft: here it was, Thanksgiving Day, and Kowalczyk was stuck in a stranger's house, far from his own family, technically on duty even as he nibbled diffidently at a pile of stuffing.

"Tell me, Kowalczyk. Have you had a chance to talk to your own family today? If you need to excuse yourself . . ."

Kowalczyk looked up sheepishly from his plate. "No, thank you. That's not necessary. I don't . . . well, I don't have a family exactly. I'm not married, and my folks passed away a few years back. You'll have to excuse me if I seem a little overwhelmed at all this family stuff."

"Overwhelmed? Please. I'm sure I speak for all of us when I say you're more than welcome to consider yourself an honorary Taft for the duration of the holidays. Rachel, Trevor, what say you?"

Trevor lowered his napkin. "Of course! From what I hear, you and Bill were fast friends anyway."

"Indeed," bellowed Taft, "the man shot me!" The table erupted in laughter. "Thank the stars Kowalczyk has lousy aim, otherwise you might be eating *me* right now for dinner!"

At that moment Abby's voice came from the direction of the living room. "Grandpa, come here! You're on TV! You're on TV!"

They left the table and went into the living room, where Abby sat, her finger pointed at the television. "I told you so!"

On the screen was the image of a man—a stout man, alarmingly so—wearing a shoddy false mustache and beaming like an imbecile. He looked worryingly familiar. And, indeed, words then appeared over the picture: PRESIDENT KANE. Taft raised a quizzical eyebrow at Rachel. "And who is this?"

She sighed. "Well, you were going to see it eventually. That's Orson Welles."

"And that signifies what, exactly?"

Rachel took a deep breath. "In the forties—the 1940s—Orson Welles was a filmmaker who wanted to make the greatest movie American cinema had ever seen. *Would* ever see. He wanted to fictionalize the life story of a man, a tragic larger-than-life man, who scaled the very top of the ladder of society only to fall apart and lose everything. Through this man, Welles figured he'd be telling the story of America—indeed, of the whole modern human race—in miniature."

"And this man . . . this man was me?"

Rachel coughed. "Uh, no. It was William Randolph Hearst."

"Hearst? That rapscallion? That rogue? That sorry excuse for a journalist? Why, he practically started the Spanish-American War single-handedly! Not that Teddy, in retrospect, ever seemed to mind."

"Well, that's the thing. Despite the fact that Welles's star was on the rise, no movie studio would touch the project. Nobody was willing to piss off the owner of the world's biggest news empire. Welles wasn't going to use Hearst's name, of course, but it wasn't going to be a secret that the movie was about him. Finally, though, someone agreed to finance the film—on one condition."

Taft sighed. "That Welles base his story on someone even more reviled and ridiculous than Hearst. Namely, me."

Rachel took Taft's hand. "I'm sorry."

He paced the carpet, trying to ignore the chatter from the television. "So this is my legacy? A . . . a freak disappearance and an unflattering movie?" *And the bathtub*, he couldn't bring himself to say. *We must never forget the bathtub.*

"It was more than unflattering, Grandpa. To take revenge on the studio that interfered with his vision—at least, that's how the speculation goes—Welles insisted he star in the movie himself. He gained a hundred pounds in six months, most of it thanks to booze.

And when he finally dressed as you and put himself in front of the camera, he was just a wreck. The story is a cartoon of your life, and he played your character as if he hated you personally—or at least hated that you were the unwitting symbol of his loss of artistic integrity. Not only did *President Kane* fail to become the greatest movie ever made, it went down as the worst. Welles never made another film, and he drank himself to death a couple years after its release. And—"

"And that's how the world remembers me. As a footnote to a failed filmmaker." His voice softened. "And even my family has been forced to carry that shame, all these years later."

Rachel hung her head. "Grandpa, you have to know this. The Taft family retreated from the public eye, true. We never stood up and defended you the way we should have. Maybe that was understandable, and maybe it wasn't. But here's the fact now: you are here, and so am I, and blood is thicker than anything. Whatever you choose to do with the rest of this life you've been given back, I'm there for you. We all are."

"Whatever I choose to do. That's the question, isn't it?" He stopped pacing. "Am I really part of this world? Of this family? Could I ever really be again?" Taft stood and stroked his mustache and patted his gut, full as it was with TurkEase and good old-fashioned Taft fortitude. His voice began to billow and rise like a sail filling with a sudden powerful wind. "Rachel, this long era of our family's reticence and shame is over. I won't allow my own mistakes and shortcomings to hamper you or your career any longer. What about the future? You're already a congresswoman. Who knows what Abby can someday achieve. For your sake, for hers, it's time the name Taft rang from the rafters once again."

AS A WORLD TRAVELER at the advent of the twentieth century, Taft had suffered every imaginable manner of intestinal malady. Such was par for the course: goulash-induced bloating in Budapest, parasitic irregularity in Manila, and fleeting bouts of seasickness at all points in between. Even his own recent virgin voyage on an airplane had been less than idyllic.

None of these trials, however, had inured his innards to the violent, almost vengeful incontinence brought on by Fulsom TurkEase.

By the end of the day, everyone in the house—all stricken save for Abby, who was spared from stinking indignity by the grace of God, or at least the strength of her young and hearty constitution—lay about the living room, drained of fluids and good humor.

"That," wheezed Trevor, his arms wrapped around his torso as if they were the only thing keeping his guts together, "is the last time we ever eat Fulsom anything. Let alone TurkEase."

Rachel hushed him. "Don't even *say* that word. You know what this is, right? Poetic injustice. Is there such a thing? Because that's what this feels like."

Taft laughed as audibly as his seemingly bruised insides would allow. "If anything, you've certainly convinced me of your cause. Back in my day, we were no strangers to bad food. That's why Teddy passed his agricultural reforms in the first place. But it was supposed to get better."

"Don't get me wrong, Grandpa. We've made great strides in food safety and wholesomeness in the past century. Not all food manufacturers, even the big agribusiness conglomerates, are as bad as Fulsom. But things have taken a turn for the worse. Healthy food is readily available, but companies like Fulsom make it easier for people to get addicted, for lack of a better word, to fat and salt and genetically modified ingredients. Hell, I can't even claim to be totally immune to their marketing. I mean, I've been eating Fulsom TurkEase and Sausage Saucers and Chick-n-Liks since I was a little girl. With all the research I've been doing over the past couple years, I know better than anyone. I've never met the man, but my beef with Gus Fulsom is personal. I grew up eating his company's products, and I still break down every once in a while and buy some of this, this . . . stuff." She reached over and took Trevor's hand. "We try our best to eat better, for our sake and for Abby's. But every once in a while, we just get busy and wind up on the path of least resistance."

Taft couldn't help but be reminded of himself. There had been no Fulsom Foods in his day. But the way Rachel spoke about the lack of control, the surrender to impulse, the comfort to be found in the flavors of youth . . . these he knew. All too well. He thought of Nellie, and of the ways she'd tried to guide him away from temptation.

Suddenly he sat up. Ignoring the wellspring of pressure that ballooned in every direction from somewhere near his tailbone, he drew back his shoulders and raised his voice. "This will not stand. I will help you, Rachel. This cause is as noble and worthy as any Teddy Roosevelt ever undertook. I'll do whatever I can to help you bring this crusade to the masses. So Pauline Craig wants me to appear on her television program? It is time I pick up her gauntlet and address the nation as a president does his people! It is time to purge this great nation of a great many things—starting with Fulsom's festering reservoir of corruption!"

His stomach lurched abruptly. He hoped he wouldn't be purging too literally.

Fox News Poll

What do you think of former president William Howard Taft?

Respected elder statesman: 35 percent
Forgettable and irrelevant: 27 percent
Dangerously out-of-touch loose cannon: 21 percent
Undecided: 10 percent
Imposter/hoax/fraud: 7 percent

ELEVEN

"GOOD GOD, MAN. Is all this truly necessary? Preposterous! I must look like a cut-rate Manila harlot."

Taft sat petrified in the dressing-room chair, his face a frozen flinch, as if he were under the straight razor of a bloodthirsty barber.

"No talking. You're smearing." The makeup artist fastidiously daubed his cheeks with a pigmented brush. Taft felt like a fidgeting child being scolded by a portraitist—only he was the canvas.

Susan seemed greatly amused by it all. She sat in a folding chair against the wall, her coat lying over her lap and a cup of tea balanced on top of the coat. Surely a woman of such propriety must be able to see the indignity of his current predicament, but, as Taft already knew, she took a perverse delight in seeing him bluster.

"Sorry. I suppose I should have warned you about this," she told him. "We were so wrapped up in preparing that the makeup part of being on TV completely slipped my mind."

Taft highly doubted that, but he let it lie. He had other things to worry about, for instance, the fact that this so-called makeup artist was dangerously close to sticking a brush in his eye.

"Steady now, man! I'm too pretty for an eye patch."

The makeup artist refused to laugh. Instead, he stepped back and inspected Taft's face from a fresh angle. "Let me just throw this out there, okay? You wouldn't be interested in shaving off that horrid thing, would you?"

"My mustache?"

"If that's what you're calling that thing, then yes. Your mustache."

"This mustache, I'll have you know, is the last living presidential mustache in United States history. And, furthermore, it's a symbol of both affluence and virility—and a dashing one at that, I might add." It was bad enough he'd already had to trim it.

"Oh, *sure*. My mistake." He twirled Taft's chair around to face the mirror that took up almost the entire length and width of one wall. He had to admit that the Manhattan television studio in which Pauline Craig was headquartered had a well-equipped green room. As Susan had explained, Craig often invited high-ranking politicos, military brass, and the occasional screen or singing celebrity, all of whom were accustomed to being primped and preened prior to placement in front of a camera.

Taft balked at the thought. His armpits had already dampened at the thought of having his voice and moving image broadcast live across the nation—no, the world, Susan had said—and he'd even begun to smell. Stage fright was something he'd overcome long ago; in fact, as Susan had explained the week before, Taft had become infamous as being one of the most long-winded speechmakers in the presidential pantheon. Secretly, Taft prided himself on that fact. After all, an address thoroughly thought out and exhaustively delivered left less room for vagueness or misinterpretation. Susan had insisted, however, that he not use the Craig interview to deliver a soliloquy. The attention span of the average American, she said in that odd lingo of hers, wasn't what it used to be. He must speak in what she called "sound bites." The very word made his stomach rumble.

"If you won't let me amputate that beast of a mustache, then will you at least let me trim it some more?" The makeup artist had found a small pair of shears, which he brandished menacingly in the mirror.

"Oh, all right. But if I measure a loss of anything more than ten percent of its total volume, I'll take it out of you in blood."

The makeup artist rolled his eyes and set about snipping.

"Susan," said Taft once the shears had been stashed and the makeup artist had left. "I won't argue with you about the need for this"—he waved his hands around his face—"this peacockery. But there's something unnatural about it. Do all politicians in this day and age subject themselves to such ostentatious falseness? Do masks now make the man? Are we all thespians?"

"Oh, really, Mr. Taft." Susan sipped her tea and shook her head. "When has politics *not* been theater? In any case, the makeup doesn't show on camera. It just makes you look . . . normal. More like yourself."

Taft snorted. "This century's infatuation with irony knows no bounds, does it?"

"Scoff all you want, but the outcome of at least one presidential election—between Nixon and Kennedy in 1960—was influenced by makeup. Or the lack thereof." She got up from her chair and looked more closely at Taft's freshly varnished face. "Anyway, I think it looks good on you."

"You do?"

"Absolutely. It really brings out your feminine side."

Taft let the comment slide. In truth, he was glad for the chance to banter. The previous week's worth of preparation had left his head stuffed with facts, figures, strategies, counterstrategies, and even a scorched-earth endgame should Craig blindside him with some kind of cheap stunt, as she'd done before. Her response when Susan had accepted the invitation on his behalf was cordial and professional, and even Susan had to admit she'd never been able to figure out exactly where Craig was coming from. Unlike other hosts of popular political-discussion programs, Craig tended to attract the rabidly independent, those viewers so exactly in the middle—or so far to either extreme—of the political spectrum that party affiliation had little meaning. Accordingly, her ideology was slippery. Susan admitted that she admired Craig on a strictly technical level, mostly for her almost magical ability to couch complex issues in blunt catchphrases that nonetheless managed to be vague enough to resonate with a relatively wide variety of audiences. She was envied and feared . . . and reviled by more mainstream journalists, who felt her methods and mode of delivery sounded the death knell of journalism.

Taft, for his part, felt the same about Craig as he did any journalist. She stank. Granted, he'd been cozy enough with the press during his tenures as Teddy's governor of the Philippines and secretary of war. Then again, during the latter appointment there had been no actual war. It wasn't until the first few months of Taft's presidency that he began to see journalists for what they really were: vipers, Visigoths, vandals hell-bent on poisoning a man's confidence before destroying him altogether. As a public servant sworn to uphold the Constitution, he fully realized the importance—indeed, the vital necessity—of a free press to the function of democracy. That said, in his heart of hearts, he'd have had every last one of them rounded up and pilloried if he'd been able.

As if sensing the tide of bitterness welling in his breast, Susan laid a hand on his shoulder. "Remember the first rule: don't let your emotions get the best of you. When you're out there, smile. Be polite.

Take every question, no matter how negative, as a fair and welcome one. Stick to your talking points; this is about Rachel more than anything else. Steer the conversation toward her whenever possible. Oh, and I almost forgot to pass along this little method: if you start to get nervous, look over at Pauline Craig and imagine her naked."

Taft felt his heart kick like the horses in his old White House stables.

"Excuse me?"

Susan's face was pregnant with some unreadable emotion as she opened her mouth to answer. But before she could say anything, a woman knocked on the door and cracked it open without waiting for a reply. "Mr. Taft," she said, sticking her smiling face and a beckoning finger into the room. "It's time. You're on. Let me get this mic on you. Then, please, follow me."

TAFT HAD NEVER BEEN ONE to rely on the conceit of the metaphor, but as he stepped, or rather was thrust, onto the stage of *Raw Talk with Pauline Craig*, he couldn't help but compare himself, not without chagrin, to a baby bird. His nest behind him, he felt lighter than air as he floated—as much as a man well past 300 pounds was able to float—across the carpet of Craig's set. It was far smaller than he'd imagined, and electric lights exploded in his eyes like a dozen suns. He could hear Susan's voice behind him, a harsh whisper, something about staying on course to Craig's guest chair alongside her desk. His ears roared as if a tornado tore past them, but it may have only been applause. Vertigo nearly overtook him, but just as his stomach felt ready to fly along ahead of him, his hand came to rest on the arm of the chair.

Then, silence.

A drop of sweat trickled along his temple, hung there, and then ran down his cheek and into his mustache. It felt, he estimated, as if the sweat drop's journey took several hours to complete.

Then a voice came booming midsentence into his brain.

"—you all right, President Taft?" He felt like a diver popping up to the surface amid someone else's conversation. He realized that he was President Taft. And the voice he heard was that of Pauline Craig.

"Yes, yes, I'm quite all right." He maneuvered his bulk into the chair, which seemed to have been purposefully designed to be too narrow, to make him look like a buffoon as he wedged his posterior into its tight frame. Knowing Craig even to the slim extent he did, that might well have been the case. "Just having a bit of a problem navigating all these noises and bright lights of yours."

"Not to mention the chair," came Craig's voice.

Taft sensed a faraway hum of what might have been laughter. He tried peering through the eye-piercing veil of light in front of him. The audience. Of course, he knew there would be spectators. But he could barely make them out through all this infernal dazzle. What kind of connection would he be able to make with them? He'd regularly and gladly faced down crowds ten times this size during his campaigns and administration. But he could always see their faces: face to face, like decent, civilized humans. He realized that these people were just the tip of the iceberg; millions more were watching him at home on their television sets. What was this unholy, lopsided manner of addressing people that had evolved since his day? No wonder Americans had devolved into such a vicious, petty, sarcastic lot. They no longer had to look each other in the eye.

And then there was Craig. Her face was most definitely present. High forehead, blond hair, sharp cheeks, a sagging chin that a hen might envy. She looked at him from behind her desk with a mixture of amusement and malice.

"The chair? Now that you mention it, it *is* a bit on the small side. Perhaps when your program sees some measure of success, you'll be able to afford proper furnishings."

The crowd—stocked, as Taft supposed it was, with Craig's sycophantic fanatics—laughed despite itself, then quickly hushed after a sharp look from the host. "Thank you," she said, "for that generous observation. If my ratings ever recover from your withering attack, I'll put a new chair on the top of my shopping list."

Damnation. He was already breaking Susan's first rule: don't take cheap shots. Keep it friendly, no matter what.

Taft collected himself. He grinned, the biggest, toothiest Teddy Roosevelt grin he could muster. "All in good fun, Pauline!" he said in his best approximation of joviality. Susan, as well as the show's production assistant, had told Taft to address her by her given name. "Pardon an old relic for his nervous jesting. I assure you, I'm quite grateful to be here on your program."

That seemed to mollify her. She smiled smugly. Taft knew her type. A bully to the core. Ten minutes, he told himself. For ten minutes, for Rachel, I can do this.

"President Taft, it is our honor to have you here. And I'm sure I'm speaking for all of America when I say that." A light smattering of applause followed. The audience reacted, it seemed, like trained dogs.

"All of America," he echoed. "That alone is a staggering thought to me. The America I left in 1913 had a few less states than it does now. Alaska, Hawaii . . . Why, if our current president had been born in my day, he only barely would have been an American!"

The crowd roared. He and Susan had cooked that one up during their week's preparation. Despite the spectrum of political thought, or lack thereof, that Craig's viewers encompassed, they all had one thing in common: paranoia, especially when it came to the legitimacy of anyone in power. Of course, he knew it was preposterous to doubt the validity of the president's citizenship, but he could always play his remarks off as a bit of mild ignorance, as if he were unaware of where Craig's followers stood on the issue. But now they were listening to him, and he'd bought himself some goodwill in case Craig leapt to the offensive.

And, sure enough, she already looked uncomfortable. "Why, yes, that's quite a good point you make. Although the topic of the president's birth is not one to be taken lightly."

"Indeed, Pauline, indeed. For instance, I was born in Cincinnati, and I am an Ohioan through and through." He drummed his chest with his fingers. "And where, my dear, are you from?"

Craig was clearly blindsided by the sudden reversal. "Me? New Jersey."

Taft threw an expansive expression toward the audience. "New Jersey! A splendid state. A shame about that disgraceful television show, though. You're not from the Jersey shore, are you?"

A wave of tittering swept the crowd. "Well, yes. Mr. President, let's talk about you. America wants to know all about you. The real you. Why you've come back, and what you plan to do now that you're here."

"The real me?" He patted his girth and grinned again. "As you can see, I've nothing to hide." They didn't laugh this time, but he could almost feel a glow from the crowd. Self-deprecation, he was relieved to see, was still the great equalizer. "As for what I plan to do, I haven't quite decided yet. Coming back wasn't my choice, as I know has been widely reported already. I wish I had more to add, but sadly I do not. I, however, have always been one to look toward the future."

"The future? For you, Mr. President, it seems that your descendant, Congresswoman Rachel Taft, may be exactly that. Have you spoken with her about her political plans for 2012?"

He and Susan had planned for this question. Still, he felt unclean—as he always did while telling even the smallest falsehood—by his prepared and prevaricating answer. "Rachel is her own person, of course. And, as you know, her position as an independent makes things a little trickier for her as she tests the waters."

"Not to mention a moderate," said Pauline with a hint of a sneer.

"Moderate to the extreme, let me assure you." This lady was beginning to try his amiable demeanor, but the crowd registered a few scattered hoots of approval. "If there were more people like her in government, we might have far less use as a people for political rooster yards and henhouses." His look took in the whole of Craig's stage and audience. The latter loved it, and a howl rose from the seats.

"Speaking of which, from what I understand, you kept many barnyard animals in the White House. I'm sure that made for a fair amount of dignity in the eyes of the nation."

Taft laughed along; he didn't dare let on that he couldn't quite get the gist of her joke. What domicile the size of the White House *didn't* have horses, cows, pigs, and chickens? And then he remembered: supermarkets, agribusiness, food subsidies, and surpluses. He'd picked up enough about such matters from Rachel and Susan, and it only made sense that the divide between urban and rural life had become more marked since his day. Come to think of it, he didn't remember picking up any of the pungent, familiar manure smells during his brief time at the White House, after his awakening. For a moment, he felt a quick pang of nostalgia.

Then, lost in thought and almost absently, he said, "Yes, of course, we kept animals at the White House during my administration. What's the word you use for it now? Sustainability? But that was just the way life was a hundred years ago. Unlike today, we were on a first-name basis with our food. Why, I had a prized cow pastured at my White House named Pauline! And a fine, broad-collared, milk-heavy cow she was. Pauline, I miss your rich cream and soothing company!"

Suddenly, all that could be heard throughout the studio was the buzzing hum of the lights.

Then the crowd erupted. The laughter died down quickly enough—Taft wondered if they were being prompted somehow; was there a sign he couldn't see?—and he realized what he'd just said. Of course, he was no stranger to such faux pas; Teddy had called it a gift, right up there with his long-windedness and lack of discretion. Granted, Taft sometimes loved to play dumb in pretentious company, just so he could levy such barbs, puncture an ego or two, and retreat behind his whiskers and innocence.

In this case, however, he hadn't meant to deflate Pauline Craig. Or equate her with a cow. But it was too late. Her face reddened and her eyes shot daggers. She called for a sponsor break.

An assistant ran out to touch up their makeup, thankfully if momentarily breaking the tension. After patching up their faces with the speed of a Buster Keaton film, a stagehand began to count down the remaining five seconds of the break. Craig, again composed and in total control, hissed out of the side her mouth, "I hope you like surprises, Taft."

"*And* we're back with President William Taft!" The countdown had run out, and in a split second Craig shifted from the sinister whisper to a full-throated broadcast voice. Even her posture and expression changed like an electric light being switched on. What made this woman tick? What was her game? He couldn't help but wonder, even as a knot of dread gathered in his belly.

"I want to speak more seriously about *you*, Mr. President." Order seemed to have been restored in the audience, and Taft swore there were even a few empty seats that hadn't been there before, as if certain less-obedient members had been surreptitiously ushered out during the break.

"I'm afraid I'm not quite as compelling a character as you might imagine, Pauline."

"I'd say a president by his very nature is compelling, wouldn't you?"

"Ah, that's where you may be misinformed. Compelling people is not leading them. At least not in a great democracy like ours."

"Tell me about *your* leadership style, Mr. Taft. Of course you're a Republican, but would you describe yourself these days as conservative or liberal?"

"If there's one thing time has taught me, Pauline, it's that those distinctions are shifting and devious. If, for instance, you're right-handed, do you denounce your left and leave it to wither, even if the task before you requires both?"

Pauline ignored the murmur that ran through the crowd. "That's a clever way of putting it, Mr. President, but the fact remains: left and right do indeed have hard-and-fast meanings, ideologically speaking, and those meanings do have tangible influences on policy and the fortunes of this nation."

"Yes, but this nation has its own direction, and far too many politicians claim to drive the American people forward when all they do is ride shotgun."

"An interesting choice of words for a former secretary of war."

He grinned. "At least during Teddy Roosevelt's time, we didn't lie by calling it something else. Funny enough, there was no war during my tenure as secretary."

"And that, Mr. President, is exactly my point." She glanced down at her desk, then picked up a small piece of paper and hesitated a moment. This was it, Taft thought. Then she took a breath and continued. "I'm sure you've had ample opportunity to observe the state of this nation since you rejoined us. The contrasts must be striking. There is more disenfranchisement among voters than ever before, and our economy is close to a shambles." What was this speech she was giving? Why the grandstanding? "Even the term 'progressive' has become muddled and mostly meaningless. But you were a true Progressive, with a capital *P*, weren't you?"

"I still am," he said proudly. "A Republican and a Progressive. That may seem like a contradiction today, and I certainly have no plans to affiliate myself with any party now or in the future. They don't speak for me, and I certainly don't speak for them." Now how did Craig lead him so easily off the track of talking about Rachel? He must steer back in that direction. "As my great-granddaughter the congresswoman has so bravely done, I must stake my claim as an independent. The Tafts, after all, have always been their own people and gone their own way. Even if we must do so alone."

Craig broke into a huge smile, the look of a trapper who hears the jaws snap shut. She put her elbows on her desk and rested her chin on her hands. "And what if I told you, Mr. President, that you are not alone?"

She nodded almost invisibly toward one of the stagehands. A previously dark monitor, as Susan had called it during their preparation, flared to life. It split suddenly into a square of four images, shifting rapidly from scene to scene.

Each showed a small crowd—in a bar, in a living room, in a church—clad in shirts and baseball caps, holding banners and pennants, chanting loudly. Their refrain matched the single word that adorned all their paraphernalia, and it resounded from the monitor and seemed to be picked up by the in-studio audience. A low rumble began to bubble through the air as if a geyser were about to blow: *Taft. Taft. Taft.*

"What you're looking at, Mr. President, is breaking news.

A *Raw Talk* exclusive. Our investigators have uncovered these groups—small, grassroots, spontaneous—that have sprung up across this great nation of ours, and they've gathered in dozens of spots today to watch this historic broadcast. Your coming out, as it were. They're just beginning to blog and network, and they seem to come from all walks of life and political viewpoints. But they have one thing in common: They want a new direction. They want a return to values and tradition. They want new leadership, one driven by reasonable common sense rather than ego or ideology."

Her voice swelled to a crescendo just as the audience broke into a raucous applause.

"In short, they want you."

Taft slumped in his tight-fitting chair, dumbfounded. This was not what he'd seen coming. Pauline Craig, on his side? He wasn't even sure *he* was on his side. But he couldn't deny the wash of emotion and adulation that poured over him, how alive it made him feel, even as a corner of his soul screamed out in panic and protest.

"President Taft," she announced as the monitor flashed image after image of cheering, fist-pumping Americans, "meet the Taft Party."

TAFT HAD ENDURED greased fingertips and frigid implements inserted into unmentionable places during the battery of medical examinations that followed his reawakening. It had been less than pleasant. None of those intrusions, however, compared to the anguish and indignity of the cameras.

Outside the exit of the television studio had assembled reporters in multitude, a babbling gaggle of ravenous interrogators with a battalion of cameras in tow. They yelled. They cajoled. They pleaded and promised and persisted. Some even threatened. As they did so, the inhuman lenses bore down on him like the sinister, waving eyestalks of some invader conjured by H. G. Wells. The evening air was cold, and a light snow had begun to whirl through the Manhattan twilight. In simpler times, Taft might have been swept up in poetic reverie, just watching it fall, his mind whisked far away from his worries. Tonight, though, his worries were being distorted, reflected back at him, and shoved into his face.

"Mr. Taft, did you know about the Taft Party? Is this all a stunt?"

"Are you announcing your candidacy?"

"What will you tell the GOP?"

"Have you looked into the legality of the situation?"

"Do you really think your politics are pertinent to America today?"

"How big is this Taft Party, and who's running it?"

"How does the congresswoman factor into your plans?"

"How is your health holding up? Are you on any diets?"

"What about your sex life?"

Taft wanted to roar, to somehow clear this rabble before him like rubbish in the face of a hurricane. But all he could think about was Susan standing behind him, taking shelter from the onslaught of light and heat and questions.

Before he could collect his wits, Kowalczyk was there. Within moments, a contingent of dark-suited Secret Service agents had cleared a path through the reporters. Four of them, led by Kowalczyk, flanked Taft and Susan and hustled them through the throng toward their nondescript sedan. "Everything's under control," he yelled, although his voice bore the slightest edge of distress.

They were halfway through the mob of reporters—all of them now baying in protest at being held back from their prey—when a raucous sound like a crashing surf pounded against them.

Those on Taft's left turned to look behind them. Placards and sandwich boards could be glimpsed among a new, rowdy mass of people descending on the reporters from the nearby parking lot. In the movement and confusion, it was hard to read the signs, but one word, writ large on all, was easy to discern:

TAFT.

Kowalczyk shouted into his headset, but it was no use. Bodies were jostled and epithets hurled, and seconds later the reporters were in a pitched, rabid melee with the Taft supporters. Kowalczyk and his agents pushed through, and, after many nudges to his posterior and elbows to his midsection, Taft was shoved into the open door of the sedan.

"Where's Susan?" he yelled at Kowalczyk, who was fighting to clear the are of flailing limbs so that he could close the door.

"Susan?" A flash of alarm crossed his face. "I thought she was in front of you."

"Kowalczyk! She must still be out there!" Taft grunted and strained to haul himself back out of the car.

"What do you think you're doing? I'll find her. Stay put."

"The hell I will." Exhaling deeply as if emptying his lungs would help him fit through the door, Taft lunged past Kowalczyk, who was nearly bowled over by the swift mass flying past. He could hear the agent hollering in outrage behind him as he ducked his head and plowed forward into the writhing, shouting riot.

Any number of grievances had ignited riots in Taft's time: labor, temperance, the threat of war. But as far as he'd known, no one had ever rioted over *him*. He tried to bury the pangs of guilt within his breast as he crashed into the crowd, letting his weight and inertia do most of the work.

As he did, he shouted for Susan.

His voice was swallowed by the mad crush. He couldn't tell how much fighting was going on; it seemed there were more arguments and pandemonium than actual fisticuffs, although he did notice a fair share of those as well. Occasionally, a startled face, wide with recognition, would catch sight of him, but he paid them no heed and moved forward as boldly as a locomotive.

Then, through the parted legs of a rioter whacking a cameraman with his sign—TAFT 2012!!! it screamed in huge hand-painted letters—he saw her.

Susan lay limp on the grass, her head rolling from side to side. He often forgot how petite she was, and she had never seemed as tiny and fragile as she did now. She was trying to avoid the stamp of feet that hammered all around, but he could see traces of blood on her arms and forehead.

Taft had always been big boned, even as a boy. When he'd grown to adulthood and assumed public office, much was made of his size. But he'd been an athletic youth, and the strength he'd cultivated in his adolescence had never left. That strength came surging back into his limbs as he knifed through the crowd now, throwing aside reporters, protesters, and agents like rag dolls. Nothing stood in his way. He didn't take his eyes off Susan until he'd reached her and picked her up effortlessly in his arms.

"Bill?" It was the first time, Taft realized, that she'd called him by his first name. Her eyes fluttered. She was clearly dazed, although Taft noted with a heave of relief that she had only one small cut on her face that accounted for the blood he'd seen. "Bill, did you see them? Their signs? I have to get this down. I have to . . ."

Her body lost what little tension remained. She slipped into unconsciousness.

William Howard Taft raised his great, jowled, whiskered face to the heavens and howled.

"Enough!" His voice thundered across the lot and echoed off the walls of the studio and nearby buildings, amplified by years of making speeches to large assemblies without the aid of electricity or microphones. "I said: ENOUGH!"

Taft was shocked by his own booming authority. His was the voice of a man righteously outraged, a human being in full possession of his faculties—in short, a president.

It took only a second for the mob to cease and still, stricken by awe. The few remaining pockets of conflict were squelched by those standing nearby. They all turned to look for the source of that voice.

There stood Taft, the prostrate form of Susan Weschler gathered in his arms, snowflakes falling around him and sticking to his quivering mustache, a sight both slightly comical and terrifyingly elemental.

Just then, approaching from a distance, sirens began to wail.

The Washington Post
Dec. 8, 2011

NEW YORK CITY—A new political movement made a turbulent debut last night as crowds of people bearing signs proclaiming support for a group called the Taft Party mobbed the streets outside the studio of *Raw Talk with Pauline Craig*, where former president William Howard Taft had just been interviewed in a live television broadcast. The raucous crowd, which police estimated at approximately two hundred, sent five people to New York Presbyterian Hospital with minor injuries and damaged camera equipment of several network news crews.

A spokesperson for Congresswoman Rachel Taft's office stated that the Taft Party is not affiliated with the congresswoman or William Howard Taft, her great-grandfather. She confimed that William Howard Taft's chief aide, Susan Weschler, was among those treated and released from the hospital last night.

Demonstrators described the Taft Party as a loose grassroots coalition of concerned citizens seeking to recapture a more civilized era of American democracy.

"We were just there to root for Taft," said Brian Talley, a grocer from Virginia. "It was some jerk rent-a-cop who started pushing and shoving, not the Tafties. We came in peace but, man, don't tread on us."

As the demonstration descended into chaos, former president Taft refused to take shelter behind his Secret Service detail, leaping into the thick of the confusion to assist his aide, who was knocked briefly unconscious. Taft's quick move to the center of the throng, where he called for order, was credited by many as the deciding factor in restoring peace.

"He was like an action hero," said Dee Anderson, a librarian from New Jersey and Taft Party demonstrator. "I had no idea such a big man could move so fast. What's that saying—that a president should speak softly and carry a big stick? With Taft it was more along the lines of, boom like a giant and you won't have to bother with the stick."

The Taft Party United Support Association
About Us

MISSION STATEMENT

The Taft Party came together in fall 2011 in response to the reappearance of former president William Howard Taft, which served as a clarion call to all Americans, reminding us that politics in the United States once attracted a more sensible, more decorous class of participant—and must do so again. Our mission is to gather, inform, organize, and motivate our fellow Americans to achieve a higher quality of political representation across the ideological spectrum in the 2012 election and beyond.

CORE VALUES

1. Common Sense National Policy (read more)
2. Equitable Treatment of Citizens (read more)
3. Care for the Future Shaped by the Past (read more)

EVENTS

New Year's Eve rallies—Dec. 31, 2011
Primary protests—February–March 2012
Taft Party National Convention—July 12–15, 2012

REGIONAL TAFT PARTY BLOGS & GROUPS

Mid-Atlantic—coordinator: Allen Holtz, aholtz@taft2012.com
Midwest—coordinator: Frank Lommel, flommel@taft2012.com
South—coordinator: Rev. Todd Osborne, tosborne@taft2012.com
Southwest—coordinator: Linda Beach, lbeach@taft2012.com
Northwest—coordinator: Matt Shelby, mshelby@taft2012.com
New England—coordinator: Victoria Eldridge, veldridge@taft2012.com

MORE INFO

About William Howard Taft—taft2012.com/taft

How to participate—taft2012.com/community

Signs, buttons, shirts & more—taft2012.com/store

Support the Taft Party USA—taft2012.com/donate

TWELVE

"TAFT PARTY? How can they presume to call themselves the Taft Party when *we* are the Tafts?"

Taft fidgeted furiously in the middle seat of Rachel's van, wishing by all that was holy that a ham sandwich were to be had as they drove down the highway back to D.C. Susan dozed in the back seat while, up front, Rachel poked intensely at her phone.

"Grandpa," she said, "I think you might be surprised by some of these blogs. I mean, I don't agree with everything they're saying, but they seem sincere. Some of them, well, they almost make sense."

"How so?"

"Well, some of these people are just disgruntled voters looking for something new to rally around, but some of them sound like they've really studied your administration. I'm not the expert that Susan is on the fine points of all your old issues and policies, but it looks to me like a bunch of these Tafties know their stuff. God, I can't believe they call themselves Tafties."

Taft scowled harder. "And what does my administration have

to do with anything America worries about in this day and age? I had no policy positions on your trillion-dollar national debt, on your nuclear and chemical warfare, on regulating your seven hundred broadcasting channels of television and Internet and cell phones and God only knows what else I don't know about yet."

"No," said Rachel, looking over her shoulder, "but these people know *you*. I mean, obviously they don't *know* you, but I'm kind of impressed at how thoroughly they're trying." She stared at the screen on her phone. "It looks like they're skipping over a lot of the more controversial things from your presidency, over the points that are a little too dated to translate well today. But the gist of it is there: conservative yet forward-thinking, pro-business yet pro-regulation, principled yet open to compromise. It's like America has been led to believe for so long that these are polarized ideas, ones that can't possibly be reconciled, let alone work better together.

"And now here *you* come," she went on, turning back to the highway, "straight from a time before this whole empty rhetoric of 'bipartisanship' we've all overused to the point of being meaningless. They all see something to admire in you. This woman in Florida likes that you were a thoughtful governor of the Philippines . . . this lawyer in South Carolina admires your negotiation skills, your dedication to diplomacy as the means to world peace . . . this coal miner in Wyoming, uh, seems to respect that you're, quote, not afraid to stand big and proud in your resplendent girth in defiance of the impossible Hollywood standard, unquote. Whatever it is, they're all talking about your return as being the next great inspirational force in grassroots politics. A true icon of the American people. A legacy that should inspire political action today."

Taft lowered his voice to avoid waking Susan; the last thing he needed was her jumping into the conversation with an opinion on his icon-hood. "Rachel, forgive me for being cynical, but that all sounds a little too good to be true. Did you not three weeks ago tell me that I spent my century of absence being scarcely remembered as the wretched, irrelevant laughingstock of presidential history?"

"I know. It's turned around on a dime. It's bizarre. And yet, right there, what you just did a second ago—that's the other thing: that self-deprecation of yours. These Tafties love it. All those times when you were in office and you spoke openly to the press about how reluctant you were to hold the presidency, how you couldn't wait to leave it and get back to just being a judge again. Back then, all that talk was probably political suicide on the installment plan. Never mind 'probably'; it was.

"But in hindsight? From the perspective of people today who have to put up with the twenty-four-hour news networks forcing never-ending political campaigns down our throat for three and a half out of every four years? You're the most refreshing thing any of these bloggers have ever heard of. A president who *doesn't* lust for power, or covet it once he has it. Grandpa, it may be a hundred years too late to do you the political good you needed, but, here and now, you've really connected."

Taft wondered if, perhaps, he might find that prospect more comforting if he could grasp any of that connection himself. He peered out the van's tinted window at this teeming, overbuilt, new America that flashed by. For, as things stood, his own space in this gigantically overwhelming new world still felt . . . small. Laughably, impossibly small.

Dec. 22, 2011

Dear President Taft,

It is an honor, sir, to wish a Merry Christmas—and, indeed, a Joyous Resurrection—to a long-lost fellow Bonesman. Few are the fraternities of men given the opportunity to see one of their own restored to vitality after what must surely be considered a period of true death! Were we not so humble as we are, surely we must now consider Skull and Bones to have entered an august circle of divine institutions that also includes Christianity itself.

Naturally, you are engaged in your own pursuits. Know, regardless, that you are once again considered a treasured elder brother of this proud society, and that the comforts and community of the Skull and Bones Tomb remain at your disposal whenever you may choose to take advantage.

You represent both Yale and the Bonesmen mightily, sir, and from the freshest undergraduates to the most seasoned alumni, we remain—

Yours,
The men of Skull and Bones 322

THIRTEEN

WILLIAM HOWARD TAFT had been a son, a husband, and a father; he had been a scholarly student and a robust athlete; he had been a horseback rider and an automobile driver and an enthusiastic solver of logic puzzles. But as he spoke on the telephone with Irene Kaye, a woman who had once been fifty years his junior and was now fifty years his senior, he realized just how long it had been since he'd been in a position to just ask a grandma for some kindly advice.

"Something the matter with you?" the old woman's voice crackled, and, indeed, Taft didn't know whether the crackling was the telephone connection or her aged vocal cords. "Taft, if you don't want to be in politics anymore, don't be in politics anymore."

"I fear it's not quite that simple, Irene," he said. "Were it only a matter of my own interests, I would happily agree. But I now have Rachel's career to consider as well."

She snorted. "She's a big girl. Got into Congress without you. Taft, what do you want to do?"

"I . . . I don't know. In March 1913, getting out of politics was all I could think of. You know, Irene, here's what I do know: whatever I'm to do with the remainder of my life, I need to get out there and see America. I must understand the nation once again if I'm to be part of it under any terms."

"Well, now," said the scratchy voice across the ether, "that wasn't hard, was it? Get out of there, Taft. Take a vacation."

Yes. Yes, indeed. He had once been called the motoring president, hadn't he? It was time to get back in touch with his adventuresome side.

It was time, in short, for a road trip.

CLASSIFIED
Secret Service Incidence Report
BBR2011226.004
Agent Ira Kowalczyk

At 0959, handed off the D.C. security detail to Agent Pearsall for the duration of Big Boy's cross-country road trip—said duration yet to be determined. In order to facilitate Big Boy's insistence on a mere one-man guard presence while on the road, I have equipped Big Boy with a Mark II panic button and instructed him in its emergency use. Furthermore, I have determined that we will once and for all be addressing the recognition factor.

FOURTEEN

IN THE ROOM of the cheap, out-of-the-way motel Kowalczyk had carefully scouted and snuck them into that evening, Taft sat on a shabby, cigarette-burned bedspread and watched television as if in a trance. The feature, despairingly enough, was a farcical and at times willfully offensive program called *WKRP in Cincinnati*. Save for a character known as Johnny Fever—who, Taft couldn't help but notice with envy, was almost angelically easygoing, as if under the sway of some pharmaceutical relaxant—it was horrible. Was this how Americans viewed his beloved home? Was it no longer a proud boomtown, the City of Seven Hills, but a repository for incompetent clerks and buxom floozies? He nibbled absently on a leg of fried chicken, unable to change the channel or even divert his gaze.

"What the hell are you watching?" Kowalczyk said as he opened the bathroom door and stepped back into the tiny, two-bed sleeping room. He carried a white plastic bag that Taft hadn't noticed earlier.

"*WKRP in Cincinnati*," Taft snorted. "Horrendous. Leave it to the twenty-first century to make vaudeville look dignified."

"The twenty-first century? Bill, that show is, like, thirty years old. I was a little kid when it was first on."

"Oh? Am I to believe, then, that Cincinnati is even *more* of a farce today than it was then?" He sighed. "At least this Fever fellow has a grand enough mustache."

"Uh, yeah. Funny you should mention that."

Taft looked sharply at the agent, who was pulling several small items out of the white bag. Cardboard packages; a bar of soap; a razor.

"Oh, no."

"Oh, yes. I'm sorry, Bill, but if you're serious about spending God knows how long, the two of us, wandering from state to state without a larger guard detail, then you're going to have to let me use every tool at my disposal to keep you safe. That means not Tafting it up every second of the day. And that means, the mustache comes off."

**Number of people attending the Arizona
Taft Party rally on Dec. 28:**

24,500 (estimated)

FIFTEEN

CHICAGO WAS EXACTLY as Taft remembered it: that is to say, unrecognizable. The city had been in such a state of construction and flux during his day—especially following the Great Fire in '71, when he was but a youngster—that it seemed a completely different yet hauntingly familiar place each time he visited. Today was no different. There were more roads, taller skyscrapers, and a greater profusion of people to be seen as he and Kowalczyk passed the South Side, but that was offset by the pervasive, living *spirit* of the city.

Not to mention the smell.

"Is that a hot dog vendor my nose detects?" said Taft, his face lapping up the breeze from the open passenger-side window.

"Bill, you look like a dog yourself, hanging your head out of the window like that," answered Kowlaczyk. His crown full of stubble gleamed in the afternoon sun that slanted through the windshield. Old snow lay scattered in random, filthy heaps along the roadside and the edges of parking lots. "At least we're lucky we didn't run into any blizzards. Still, you might want to roll up that window before you catch cold. After all, you have a little less of your winter coat to keep you warm." He pointed to the place where Taft's whiskers had previously bristled.

"Go ahead and laugh, Kowalczyk," Taft said dryly. "Get it all out." He did indeed feel bald without his mustache, but, in a way, the shave suited him. It was as if a great pressure had been magically hoisted away—the weight of his own image, his own identity. Since he'd shaved it off, no one had given him a second glance, not even when they'd sat in the packed truck-stop diner that morning, breakfasting on French toast and bacon as the television above their heads blared Pauline Craig's latest tirade concerning Taft.

"I almost wish I were president right now," Taft had growled, a forkful of greasy lusciousness hovering in front of his lips. "The first thing I'd do is outlaw this absurd custom of mounting televisions in every damned public space. Whatever happened to conversing with one's fellow man while in a restaurant?"

"I'm sorry, what?" Kowalczyk's glazed eyes were glued to the screen.

"See? It's a scandal, I tell you. Why did we ever fight a war for independence if we'd eventually wind up signing our lives over to this . . . this . . . idiot machine."

"Idiot *box*."

"Excuse me?"

"It's called an idiot box, Bill. And, rest assured, you aren't the first grumpy old guy who's had those thoughts." But before Taft could protest, Kowalczyk laid a finger over his lips. "Check it out. It's getting worse. Or better, depending on your warped point of view."

Sitting in the car with the sights, sounds, and smells of Chicago whizzing by, Taft didn't want to remember what they'd seen on that truck-stop TV earlier in the day. But he couldn't push it out of his mind, either; Craig, it now seemed, had fully cast off any reservations and become the most ardent, barking proponent of William Howard Taft that he'd ever remembered having. On her show that morning had been a guest named Marsha McCursky, a woman who identified herself as a labor leader, although Taft had no idea what kind of labor she represented. She spoke in vague, rhetorical terms about things like a return to true Progressive values—she stressed the capital *P*—and something she called "protoconservatism," whatever the hell that was supposed to mean. She warned of the dominance of corporate power and influence in American society. At the same time, she seemed to be almost against corporate regulation. If Taft heard her nebulous platitudes correctly, she seemed to be saying that less regulation would give the government less opportunity to sneak into bed with the lobbies, and that it would prevent corporate consolidation by lessening covert government backing of such activity.

The backward logic of this idea made his head spin—even more so considering that it was being foisted on the public as his own legislative legacy. And what rubbed him even rougher was the "TAFT 2012!" slogan that had been emblazoned across McCursky's shirt, not to mention the shirts of at least two people Taft had seen in the diner at the next booth over.

But that wasn't all that was on his mind. Even earlier that morning, back in the hotel room, Taft had unzipped his small leather bag of toiletries to find . . . himself. That is, Abby's Taft doll. Not her old rag doll, but the fancy new plastic one—the one that had come in a box labeled "Presidential Action Figure Special Edition!"—that he'd gotten her for Christmas. It seemed she had smuggled it inside his luggage, along with a note that read: "Dear Grandpa, I hope you have a nice trip. Here's someone to keep you company. Don't forget about us. We'll miss you. Love, Abby."

The note was in the little girl's shaky handwriting, but he could hear her voice saying the words as if she were on his lap.

Her precocity knew no bounds! A Taft to the core. Yet, for some reason, Abby's small, sweet gesture only made him feel more moody than buoyed.

It didn't help that Chicago, as magnificent as it still seemed to be, held a bittersweet aftertaste for Taft. It was there in the summer of 1912 that the Republican National Committee had awarded him the party's nomination, a decision overwhelmingly unfavorable to Teddy Roosevelt, who had decided to try to take the White House back from Taft. Taft had stayed in D.C. during the convention in Chicago, but Teddy—in a fiery breach of protocol, which should have surprised no one—appeared in person and finally broke all friendship ties with Taft. "We stand at Armageddon, and we battle for the Lord," Teddy had cried to his dwindling faithful, casting Taft as Satan in his thespian drama-mongering. Taft tried to keep the party together after that, pledging conciliation rather than alienation. But one thing he couldn't do was reach out to Teddy, not after he began his preposterous run as a third-party candidate, which ultimately split the GOP vote, making way for wooden Woodrow Wilson to waltz right in. That summer in Chicago back in '12 was, by all outward appearances, Teddy Roosevelt's Waterloo. But it was also Taft's—and, as he'd come to understand it, the beginning of the end of Republican progressivism as a whole.

"Bill? You okay?" Kowalczyk's voice broke him out of his cloudy daydream. He realized that he'd pulled Abby's Taft doll out of his jacket pocket—just so the white-whiskered head was peeking out—and had been staring at it.

"Yes, I'm fine. It's just . . . my mind is wandering, that's all."

"I'll say," Kowalczyk said, opening his door and putting on his sunglasses. "We've been parked in front of this hot dog joint for five whole minutes already, and you haven't even twitched a muscle."

Taft looked at the comically rotund head of the doll made in his image, the vapid grin sculpted into his tiny plastic face. "To be perfectly honest, Kowalczyk, I seem to have lost my appetite."

Kowalczyk stared at him with an unreadable expression. He shut the car door. "Know what? I've got an idea." He put the key back in the ignition and shifted into reverse. "Over the past five days we've eaten at Friendly's, IHOP, T.G.I. Friday's, Buca di Beppo, and half a dozen deli counters. You've made small talk with plenty of 'real Americans eating real meals.' How about we try something different for a change?"

"Sir, I am all ears."

"If all those food shows on TV are true, Chicago is some kind of mecca for fancy dining. Let's try to put something gourmet in your belly. Bill, have you ever heard of molecular gastronomy?"

Usage of Organic vs. Factory-Treated Ingredients in American Kitchens, 2010

Produce: 12 percent organic
Dairy: 6 percent organic
Grains: Less than 4 percent organic
Meat: Less than 4 percent organic
Other: N/A

SIXTEEN

AS THEY FOLLOWED the maître d' past gaily dressed yet uncomfortable-looking diners, the harsh light, sharp angles, and cold chrome of Atomizer made the place feel more like a clinic than a restaurant. When Taft said as much to Kowalczyk, he stood corrected: "A clinic? More like a laboratory."

Kowalczyk was right. After determining the location of the highest-rated molecular-gastronomy bistro in Chicago, he and Taft had gussied themselves up as best they could with the contents of their suitcases and headed toward downtown. Once inside, they felt as though they'd stepped into another world. The walls were covered in slate gray geometric panels backlit by neutral neon. A frigid sterility glinted off the oddly hexagonal tables, and a sheen of artificiality clung to everything. And then there was the maître d': pale, white haired, and clad in a spotless beige boilersuit, he appeared both adolescent and ancient.

"What's with the Warhol look?" Kowlaczyk whispered behind a cupped hand, but the reference was lost on Taft. "Oh, never mind. Christ, can you believe this place?"

Indeed, he could not. As the maître d' seated them, he lifted the flap of a puffy rectangular purse slung from his shoulder. A wisp of vapor uncoiled from the open bag. "Your menus, sirs." He handed them each a translucent pink, paper-thin wafer on which words had somehow been etched. It was barely legible.

"Could you perhaps just tell us the specials of the day?" said Taft as he took the menu. It felt cold and slick between his fingers.

The maître d' sniffed. "Specials?" He swept a hand in front of him as if he were about to take a bow. "Everything at Atomizer is scientifically formulated to be special."

Taft raised an eyebrow. "I'll say." At that moment, he felt something trickle down the inside of his shirtsleeve.

"Uh, Bill," said Kowalczyk. "These things are melting."

"What in Hades—" Kowalczyk wasn't joking. The unusual menus had begun dissolving in their hands. Two large pieces had already fallen off, landing on the table in a puddle of pink, watery goo.

"The menus," the maître d' informed them, "are edible. Go ahead, try it."

Taft cautiously licked one of his fingers. It tasted vaguely of berries. "Hmm, yes," he grumbled. "Now if I could only read the damn thing."

The maître d' smirked. "Your server will be along shortly."

"So this is—what did you call it—malevolent gastronomy?" Taft said as soon as the white-haired host was out of earshot.

"*Molecular.* It's the hottest new thing. Or at least it was five years ago. I think."

Taft dragged a fingertip through the pool of melted menu on the table, which had already started scabbing into some kind of taffylike substance.

"Come on, Bill, keep an open mind. You said you wanted to

get a taste of the real America, right? Well, this is what the people are eating."

"Hmph. The wealthy and pretentious, perhaps. But the people?" He glanced around at the haughty, miserable-looking patrons seated nearby. "I doubt it."

When the server reappeared a minute later, all that was left of Taft's menu was a small, smudged shard that smelled faintly of hard candy. Cupping it in his palm, he squinted and said, "I suppose I'll be having the Reverse-Osmosis Salmon S'mores. Whatever on God's green earth that's supposed to mean."

The server returned five minutes later with two martini glasses full of carbonated foie gras and a note scrawled on a crumpled napkin. The waiter stood at attention as Taft unfolded and read it to Kowalczyk: "Dear Taft party, your presence is requested at the chef's table. Please bring your cocktails and follow your server. Regards, Castro Cozmos."

"Did he capitalize *party*?" Kowalczyk asked, his face innocent.

"Don't even joke," said Taft with a sigh. "Well then. I suppose it was too much to think we'd escape the prying eyes of the public, even after the removal of my most distinguishing—and, might I add, distinguished—feature." He stood up, sniffed his fizzing glass of liver paste, wrinkled his nose, and emptied it into Kowalczyk's. "In any case, we shan't be ungracious guests. Shall we?"

CASTRO COZMOS, CHEF and proprietor of Chicago's acclaimed and trend-setting Atomizer, stood in the restaurant's cluttered, chaotic kitchen with his arms buried to the elbows in a white industrial bucket full of a pulpy, fibrous, indeterminably meatlike dough. Pale and pasty, he appeared to be made from the same substance as the one he was kneading. The smell was rich and almost rancid; Taft recognized it from somewhere, but he was too busy swallowing back a bit of bile to wonder about it. Kowalczyk, too, turned slightly green in the presence of the odor, but he remained quiet and put on a wan smile as Castro looked up from his bucket and grinned hugely at them as the maître d' led them into the kitchen.

"Mr. President! I'll wash off and be with you in just a second. Please, have a seat over there at the chef's table." He stuck his chin out in the direction of a small, rickety table in the middle of the kitchen surrounded by folding chairs and a steady stream of bustling yet slovenly groomed cooks.

The server pulled out their chairs. Taft's shuddered under his weight. "Careful there," quipped Kowalczyk as he took his own seat and pointed at Taft's belly. "I don't think that thing was made for multiple occupants."

"That's quite a bold affront, coming from a bald fellow."

Kowalczyk rubbed his palm over his scalp. "Oh, this? Remember, Bill, I'm a Marine. This was my hairstyle for years."

"Really? Is that how they deloused you?"

"Gentlemen!" Castro Cozmos stepped up to the table, turned a chair around, and plunked himself down. He smelled of cigarettes and, of course, the gloppy meat-starch he'd been manhandling. With a grubby towel he wiped his forearms and then began cleaning under his yellowish fingernails. "Welcome to Atomizer." He shook hands with Taft and then Kowalczyk. "Castro Cozmos, molecular gastronomist."

"Kowalczyk. Hungry man."

A laugh bubbled up on Castro's unshaven face. "Hungry! I like hungry. I'll warn you right now, though: here at Atomizer, we're not concerned with anything so pedestrian as filling stomachs."

"So it's all about taste over substance?" Kowalczyk said, grinning.

"Taste? Why, that's even more boring." He pointed toward a line of nearby sous-chefs, each in some stage of unpacking, kneading, slicing, or microwaving a particular packaged food product. "Atomizer isn't about flavor or sustenance. We're all about the *process*."

Castro snapped his fingers and waved at a cook from the line. "Phillip! Bring us over an order of the, oh, the Deconstructed Nacho Roe."

Phillip nodded and removed a bowl from the nearest microwave, added a few shots of some powdered substance, then dumped it all into a machine set up on a wheeled cart. With the cord trailing behind, he pushed the cart over to their table. When he pressed a button on the side of the machine, it started whirring and purring like a dervish.

"What you see here," said Castro, patting the vibrating cart, "is a centrifuge." A moment later Phillip switched off the contraption and spooned a few hills of miniscule, iridescent yellow globules onto the plates in front of them. "We take your average, off-the-shelf cheese sauce, add a secret recipe of eleven binding agents, fillers, flavor enhancers, and emulsifiers, and . . . *voilà*! Caviar-shaped nacho cheese!" He picked up a piece of triangular, tortilla-shaped bacon from a platter Phillip had supplied and dug into the sticky pearls of goo.

Taft reached for the bacon, then stopped himself. "And where does the cheese sauce come from? Is it made from scratch?"

"*Scratch*?" Castro spat the word. "Mr. President, please! Nothing at Atomizer is made from scratch. That's our whole philosophy and branding strategy! With all due respect, old buddy, we're living in the twenty-first century. 'From scratch' is a quaint and outmoded notion. Atomizer is all about engineering the engineered, manipulating the manipulated. *Processing the processed*."

Kowalczyk sat with his arms crossed. "Any chance I could get a burger?"

Castro snapped his fingers again. "A burger! Of course. Phillip?"

Half a minute later, a sandwich arrived and was placed before Kowalczyk. "This is the world-famous Atomizer, the very burger our restaurant is named after. Please, enjoy."

Kowalczyk stared at his plate. Sitting there, steaming and sweating, was some object that roughly resembled a hamburger. He picked up his fork and lifted one end of what might have been the top bun. Instead of a patty of meat, the bottom bun held a mess of wet confetti that stank of death and ketchup.

"Allow me to explain," said Castro. "We don't use anything as conventional as ground beef in our Atomizer. What you see before you is a chemically formulated, aerated amalgam of beef, cheese, and toppings. Would you like a little more?" Before waiting for an answer, he turned to Phillip and said, "Let's make this a Double Atomizer for Mr. Kowalczyk here!"

Phillip left and hurried back with an unlabeled aerosol can. He lifted the top bun of Kowalczyk's burger, shook the can, aimed it, and pressed the nozzle. Out flew a slurry of burger-matter that landed on the bun like some brownish, curdled, flesh-scented snow.

Kowalczyk coughed. "Well, ah, that's something else, I'll give you that. And I'd love to try it. But, you know, I'm a vegetarian."

"Since when are you—" Taft started to protest, but Kowalczyk kicked him into silence under the table.

Castro winked at him. "There's the beauty of it: the meat and cheese we use is so processed, before and after we receive it here in the kitchen, that the FDA has qualified our food as legally vegan! Granted, the government has some pretty loose definitions of words like *vegan*, *organic*, and *natural*. And hopefully it'll stay that way, assuming Mr. Fulsom has his way."

"Fulsom?" Taft's stomach lurched at the name. "The TurkEase manufacturer?"

"Yes! The one and the same. We have an exclusive contract with Gus Fulsom. In fact, he's one of the silent partners here at Atomizer. Everything on our menu is made from Fulsom-brand products. It's funny you should mention TurkEase. That's what I was mixing up when you came in. The Atomizer buns are made of it—not wheat, but turkey byproducts!"

Taft and Kowalczyk traded pained glances, memories of their disastrous TurkEase Thanksgiving swimming up into the backs of their throats.

"See," Castro went on, munching on Kowalcyzk's untouched Atomizer, "Fulsom supplies the most processed foods we can get a hold of, and at a significant discount. In return, we help counter some of the stigma against processed food in general—and what better way than by reimagining it as haute cuisine! In essence, we're doing something very noble here. And do you know what that is?"

Taft gulped. "Keeping this stuff off the streets?"

"No, Mr. President," he said, his mouth full and his eyes narrow. "We're extracting purity. Purity from corruption."

"Purity from corruption? Pardon me for laughing, but I know a good many politicians who have said, in essence, the same thing. And they were all snakes."

"Well, I can assure you, Mr. President, that Gus Fulsom is no snake. In fact, you should meet him someday. Who knows? You two might even have more in common than you realize." Castro let his words hang in the air before calling over Phillip one last time. "Box up a couple more Atomizers for Mr. Taft and his friend! And throw in a couple plates of Nacho Roe and Salmon S'mores."

Castro rose from his seat and jabbed his thumb toward the other end of the kitchen. "In any case, I have to get back to work.

Pardon me for hijacking you two, but we haven't had a president eat here in, oh, at least three weeks. Let alone one of such . . . moral appetite."

With that, Castro left them. Taft and Kowalczyk looked at each other, glanced at Phillip stuffing two enormous plastic bags full of Atomizer fare, and bolted toward the door.

PAULINE CRAIG: Welcome back to *Raw Talk* with me, Pauline Craig. As you know, William Howard Taft recently appeared on our show, and we broke the story that day that everyday Americans have begun to rally around the former president and his traditional, rock-solid values—have even gone so far as to start a so-called Taft Party to promote those good, strong, heartland American ideals. Today, we're going to start getting to know those enthusiastic Taft supporters. With me in the studio is Allen Holtz, a hardworking electrician from Richmond, Virginia. Hello, Allen!

ALLEN THE ELECTRICIAN: Pleased to meet you, Pauline.

PAULINE CRAIG: Let's start by talking a little about you. What's your story, Allen?

ALLEN THE ELECTRICIAN: Aw, I'm just your average, blue-collar, middle-class guy. I've worked as a journeyman electrician my whole life. I've voted Democrat, sometimes, and I've voted Republican. Ever since I was a kid, I always tried my best to figure out what the issues are, you know, what direction American ought to be going in, that sort of thing. But the older I got, the more confused I became.

PAULINE CRAIG: And how has this recession affected you? As an independent contractor, do you have access to health insurance? A retirement plan?

ALLEN THE ELECTRICIAN: Well, you know, Pauline, I haven't had good health insurance for a bunch of years. Like I said, I'm a blue-collar guy just trying to get by. I managed to quit smoking on my own a few years ago, with the Fulsom GiveItUp Gum, so that's something, even though I guess you can see it stains my teeth something awful and I can't afford the dentist either.

PAULINE CRAIG: And that's the kind of trade-off Americans have to make these days, isn't it? You can have the healthy body or you can have the clean teeth, but God help you if you can't afford to pay top dollar for both.

ALLEN THE ELECTRICIAN: Yeah, but you know, don't feel sorry for me. I'm glad things weren't easy for me in this life. Things aren't *supposed* to be easy. You have to work, and you have to earn. But let me also say this: we're all in this together. Do you know what I mean? Every American is my brother or my sister. I'm happy to do my part; I'm happy to pay my dues to my nation. And hey, if my neighbor is happy, if he's doing better than I am, well, I'm glad somebody is. And that's why Taft is my man. Taft has common damn sense, if I'm allowed to say that on TV. He's not for anybody special; he's for everybody. Like presidents used to be, before it all got so damn ugly.

PAULINE CRAIG: Allen, you've spent the past few weeks talking with your neighbors, your clients, your fellow Americans. What does the Taft Party have to offer?

ALLEN THE ELECTRICIAN: Well, Pauline, you know, I don't think it's any accident that William Howard Taft is back with us. I don't want to start talking divine providence or anything, but is it a *coincidence* that he came back just as his great-granddaughter, uh, Rachel Taft, started making waves in the government?

PAULINE CRAIG: We've heard people say that Congresswoman Taft has been carrying on President Taft's great legacy of level-headed independence. Of sensibility and balance—of forward-thinking conservatism. What do you think? Should William Howard Taft use his newfound popularity to advise the congresswoman? Should the Taft Party recruit her to seek higher office this election cycle? As green as she is on the national stage, should Congresswoman Taft forget about the typical progression of House to Senate to Cabinet and just run for president in 2012?

ALLEN THE ELECTRICIAN: No, no. I mean, the congresswoman is great, she's a go-getter—a free thinker—she's a real Taft. She's got a great future. But, like you said, Pauline, I've been talking with people all over, all these other Tafties who really get what it's about. We're all different; we come from every point on the political, whaddayacallit, spectrum, but there's one thing we unanimously agree on. Taft is the man. Taft is America, from when America was still proud of itself. We need Taft. If we have to, we need to *draft* Taft.

SEVENTEEN

THE BONES OF Chicago were intact and recognizable as Taft wandered with Kowalczyk past renovated storefronts and sporadic pockets of aging nightlife. But new flesh had grown up around it: more concrete, more steel, more glass. Taft patted his belly, which was now grumbling. Kowalczyk heard it. "Maybe we should've just stuck with the hot dogs, huh?" Kowalczyk said.

"Way ahead of you, my good sir." Up ahead, a neon sign in the shape of a bun-clad wiener blinked yellow and red in the window of a small establishment tucked between a tobacco shop and some sort of nightclub. "Despite the lateness of the hour, it appears our salvation is at hand."

Kowalczyk groaned but matched Taft's quickening pace. "I never thought I'd see the day where I'd be looking for a hot dog to wash the bad taste out of my mouth."

The first thing that hit Taft when he opened the door to Herbert's Dogs wasn't the smell of frankfurters. It was the smell of something burning.

"Hey, guys, sorry. I was just, uh, doing inventory." A young man, wire thin with unkempt black hair and bulging eyes, came out from the back room and took his place behind the counter. "Welcome to Herb's. What can I do you for?"

Taft chuckled. "Inventory, indeed. Are you Herbert?"

The man grinned. The tang of smoke seemed to emanate from him. "Um, there isn't any Herbert. I'm Rob. First time here?"

"You might say that." Taft peered up at the grimy, yellowed plastic of the backlit menu that hung above Rob's head. "What's your specialty, sir?"

The young man stepped out from behind the cash register and bade them to sit down at one of the dingy-clothed tables. He was wearing a T-shirt emblazoned with some monstrous horned skull and logo that read MOTÖRHEAD. "You just leave that to me. On a scale of one to ten, how hungry are you?"

Taft spread his arms. "Need you ask?"

He nodded appreciatively and then turned to Kowalczyk. "You?" Kowalczyk wrinkled his nose and held up two fingers. Rob shrugged. "Suit yourself. You guys just sit tight. A dozen Bombers and two buckets of nacho fries, coming up."

Before Taft or Kowalczyk could protest or even ask what a Bomber was, Rob disappeared into the kitchen, leaving a lingering whiff of illicit smoke.

"Well, I guess we'd better just sit back and enjoy the ride." Kowalczyk swept a tangle of discarded straw wrappers from a grimy booth and slung himself into it. "I could eat a horse at this point—assuming it wasn't packaged in a Fulsom Beef Jerky wrapper."

Taft joined him. He was too exhausted to bother complaining about the absurdly small space between table and seat. He leaned over as best he could. "If I didn't know better, I'd say this Rob fellow was inebriated."

Kowalczyk grunted. "Well, definitely under the influence. He's *high*, Bill."

"Yes, that's exactly what I'm saying. Although what kind of hooch he's high on, I am entirely at a loss."

Kowalczyk chuckled. "Not booze. Pot."

"A pot of what?"

"Bill, the guy's been smoking pot. Can't you smell it? Pot. Weed. Reefer. Marijuana."

"Ah, yes. That would explain it then." Bill heard an eruption of sizzling come from the back of the eatery. It smelled and sounded like a heart being thrown on Satan's own brazier.

"Doesn't that, I don't know, freak you out or something?"

"Why would it? It's far from the most reputable indulgence, I'll admit. Not that I've ever tried it myself. Have you?"

"Well, not in a long time. They give you so many piss tests in the Secret Service, you might as well hook up a catheter that drains straight into the head office. But back up a second—you're not uptight about pot? I just figured that, you know, being president and all, not to mention that you're, you know . . ."

"The oldest man on earth?"

"Yeah, right, that. I'm embarrassed that my history is so rusty, but wasn't marijuana totally illegal in your time?"

Taft smiled. "Your history is indeed rusty. Remember, I come from the age of the Prohibition movement. There were all manner of people and organizations obsessed with telling America what it should or shouldn't eat, drink, think. Oh, the tiffs Nellie and I would have over the subject! And from what I've come to understand, Prohibition is long past, but that mentality persists."

"So what was your take on it?"

"That's a complicated question. As much as I hate to admit it, sometimes you must pick your battles when you're in office or trying to get there, especially when it comes to political expediency.

Let's just say my views on the matter definitely evolved, and I tried to edge near the center of the debate as much as possible, if you don't mind the oxymoron."

"Uh, no, I don't mind. But weren't you a judge before you got mixed up in politics?"

"I was. But being a judge is easy. You side with the law, any law, even if personally you don't agree with it. If, that is, you're a good judge. And you side with it by deciding its most germane and just interpretation."

"Hmm. So you bend the law as far as it will go—and that makes it stronger."

Taft gave Kowalczyk a stern look. Then he laughed. "A great legal mind trapped among the rank and file of the Secret Service!"

"Hey, screw you, buddy. Seriously, though. How do you feel about, I don't know, the war on drugs and all that?" From the kitchen, the crudest, most obnoxious music imaginable began to pour out. "It's a different world, in case you needed a painful reminder."

Taft looked at his belly and shrugged. "The war on drugs. I've read about it. Sorry to answer rhetorically, but who am I to judge what someone else puts in his body?"

As if waiting for those very words to be said, Rob hurried out of the kitchen with a steaming pail in each hand and a large platter balanced on top. "Your nacho fries," he said, depositing the buckets on the table between them. Judging from its odor, the gooey, orange substance may have once had congress, albeit brief, with some distant relative of cheese. Then he set down the platter. "And one dozen Bombers, with an extra thrown in, on the house."

Taft couldn't recognize a single thing on the palm-sized buns. Meat of some species protruded in dripping shreds from the edges of the sandwiches. Slices of melted cheeselike matter, the same color as the glop that coated the French fries, swam in some iridescent commingling of sauces and gravies. Sliced vegetables, already wilted beyond recognition, made a token appearance. Something else, though, lurked under the bun—something pale and rubbery.

"Rob, if I may ask one small question." Taft pointed at the Bomber. "Is that what I think it is?"

Rob's face broke out in confusion. "Can you, uh, be more specific?"

Taft nudged the rubber substance with his fingernail.

"Oh, yeah, totally!"

"A fried egg."

"Oh, no. It's not an egg. It's the *bomb*! The bomb in the Bomber! All natural, all handmade. Organic junk food, dude!"

With that, he flipped the "Open" sign and began wiping down the nearest table. Over his shoulder he said, "You guys are my last customers, so take your time. I've got to clean up and get ready. It's New Year's Eve—2012, dudes! It's gonna be a fucking insane year. Mayan prophecies and the big election and shit. I can feel it. Just as long as those crazy Taft assholes don't turn the clock back a hundred years."

"Actually," said Taft, pointing at the mountain of untouched Bombers and uttering a sentence he didn't often have cause to use, "could you kindly wrap these up to go? And one other thing: where exactly is the best place in the neighborhood to celebrate New Year's Eve?"

"Wait a second, Bill," said Kowalczyk, but Taft held up a hand.

Rob pumped his fist, sending water from his cleaning rag spraying everywhere. "Yeah, man, that's the spirit! I'd recommend the bar next door, the Whole Hog. At least that's where I'll be most of the day tomorrow."

"How heavy-handed are their barkeeps?"

A serious look passed over Rob's face. "Oh, very. Shit, how about I meet you dudes over there tomorrow? Noon sound good? There's some serious drinking that needs to get done."

Taft looked at Kowalczyk, who was mouthing the word "no."

"Yes. We'll meet you there. I'm Bill, and this here is Kowalczyk."

"Pleased to make your formal acquaintance," said Rob. Taft couldn't tell if he was mocking him. He picked up the pails and piles of food and headed back to the kitchen to wrap them. "Oh, one more thing. You guys like punk rock, right?"

FROM THE DESK OF REP. RACHEL TAFT (Ind.–OH)

To-do list—Sat. 31st

—Disconnect phones on all future holidays.

—Do not trust people whose last names are "the Electrician."

—Decide whether I can afford to let these people co-opt my name without my participation, Wm Howard or not.

—Speaking of which. Grandpa, for the love of Pete, pick up your phone.

EIGHTEEN

KOWALCZYK HAD TRIED to argue him out of it, of course. But the more of a hoot he raised, the more Taft was convinced it was a perfectly prudent idea to get completely soused in a seedy Chicago bar on New Year's Eve day. After rising at their hotel late in the morning—and finding a much-needed proper breakfast—they headed to the Whole Hog.

In the daylight, the block that housed Herbert's and the Whole Hog was far grimier than Taft remembered. When he told Kowalzcyk as much, the former agent said, "This is the real Chicago. The real America. I thought that's what you were looking for?"

"You're in a lovely mood today."

"Yeah, well, I'm getting dragged to some shithole to spend New Year's wet-nursing a soon-to-be-bawling-in-his-beer ex-president. And this whole little state-of-the-union trip of yours is starting to grind me down." He kicked at a stack of fast-food trash that lay piled on the vomit-stained sidewalk outside the bar. "The economy's getting sucked down the plumbing, and people have had their spirit beaten out of them thanks to all these wars and bailouts and terrorist—ugh. I don't want to sound like a doomsayer or anything, but this nation is on the skids."

At that moment, the door to the bar burst open. A detonation of noise and stink flew out—along with a human being.

It was Rob.

"See here, are you all right?" Taft and Kowalcyzk picked the young man up by either arm. He was limp and babbling in their grasp.

In the open doorway stood a woman. She was six feet tall if she was an inch, ample bodied, with tattooed arms and a grubby pink tank top. Her blond hair was in braids fit for a Valkyrie. She appeared to be well into her forties, despite the fact that a picture of a cartoon kitten adorned the front of her shirt. "You know this guy?" she asked coolly.

"Yes, we do, as a matter of fact," said Taft.

"Great. Can you take care of him? Good kid. Name of Rob. Works next door. But he's been in here since we opened at eight, and he's already three sheets to the goddamn hurricane. Someone needs to teach the boy a lesson at some point, and my tough love sure as hell doesn't seem to be helping."

Between them, Rob yelled, "Samantha, is that you? 'Nother round, please. And drinks for my two friends here."

Samantha put her hands on her hips and cocked her head. "Hey, dumbass. We're not even inside the bar anymore. Why in the hell I enable your behavior, I'll never know."

Rob lifted his chin as best he could and flashed his teeth. "'Cause you're my big sister, that's why! Plus, my money is good. What kind of a bartender are you, anyway, refusing service on New Year's?"

She rolled her eyes. "One who's too old to put up with bullshit." Then she exhaled and stepped aside, waving. "All right.

Bring him in, guys. I'll make one try to pour a pot of coffee down his throat. But you have to hold him while I do it. *And*," she added, giving Taft a rock-hard look, "he's your responsibility for the rest of the day. Now, get your asses inside. What are you doing hanging out on the sidewalk, anyway? It's cold as hell out here."

THERE MAY HAVE once been walls inside the Whole Hog, but not anymore. Rather, the bar's two main rooms were bordered by layers of handbills and posters so thick, the whole place resembled some human-sized wasps' nest. Not a sliver of sunlight leaked in.

A bar twenty yards long stretched along one end of the first room; the other was filled with lopsided tables and ill-matched chairs. As Taft walked deeper into the pit of the place, he felt the soles of his shoes sticking to the floor.

"Lovely establishment you've got here, Samantha," said Kowalczyk.

"Sam." She pointed at Rob, who had propped himself up on a barstool—presumably the one he'd just been removed from. "He's the only one who gets to call me Samantha." After sliding behind the bar and pouring a mug of coffee thick enough to patch asphalt, she turned to Taft and Kowalczyk. "And since we're on the subject of names, who the hell are you two?"

After introducing themselves, Taft and Kowalczyk ordered drinks ("Wait, let me guess, a can of Olde Style for you," Sam had teased Taft with a good-natured guffaw) and took stools next to Rob at the bar.

"So, what brings you to Chicago?" Sam set out bowls of peanuts, pretzels, and popcorn, which Taft eyed for an eternal five seconds before digging in.

"What gave us away?" he said around a mouthful of salt.

"Please. I'll give it to you both, though. You're Midwesterners at least."

"We're just passing through, actually," said Kowalczyk. Then he nudged Taft with his elbow. "This one here wanted to party a little, so here we are."

"Party? You came to the right place, my friends." Sam stared out at the half-full room of tables. It was populated by men and women dressed in every imaginable permutation of denim, flannel, and leather. Their hairstyles were outrageous or merely unkempt to the point of ill hygiene. Their language—what little Taft could hear of it, anyway—was no less filthy.

"What is that racket coming from that coin-operated phonograph?" he asked Sam with a swallow of Olde Style and a wince. "Is that what passes for music in here? No offense, but that man singing sounds like he's being keelhauled through a school of sharks."

"It's the Dead Kennedys," cut in Kowalczyk.

"Excuse me?" Even in the brief time Taft had known the name since Susan had taught him of the Kennedy assassinations, it had come to take on a haunted meaning for him. He chugged down the rest of his foul-tasting brew.

"They're an old punk band, Bill. I know, I know. A Secret Service agent who likes the Dead Kennedys. Sue me."

Sam raised an eyebrow. "Secret Service, huh? Anyone around here need protecting that I ought to know about?"

Taft interrupted smoothly. "Young Rob here seems to need protection. From himself, if no one else." While they had been talking, Rob—apparently far more alert than he appeared to be—had reached across the bar and gotten his hands on some bottle of spirits or another, which he was now tipping into his mug of coffee.

Sam snatched it out of his hands. "Okay, buddy. You'd better sober up. You've only got four more hours before you need to start loading in."

"Loading in?" asked Taft. "Does Rob work here, too?"

"Work here? He barely works anywhere." She tossed the contents of Rob's mug down the drain and poured him a fresh cup. "No, Rob's the artistic one in the family. He's in the band."

"And which band would that be?"

"Let me guess—he didn't tell you. Typical. It's the old bait-and-switch. I hate to break it to you, but Rob didn't ask you over here because he thinks you're cool dudes. He was just hoping you'd get drunk enough to stick around for the show. See, he gets paid a percentage of the bar tonight. He's the lead singer of the band that's playing this evening. A special New Year's Eve set from Chicago's own Lousy Kissers." She slammed down two fresh beers in front of Taft and Kowalczyk. They made an ominous thunk. "You *are* sticking around, though, right?"

Fox News Poll, New Year's Eve

Who would you name as the 2011 newsmaker of the year?

William Howard Taft: 53 percent
Casey Anthony: 23 percent
Donald Trump: 19 percent
Other: 5 percent

NINETEEN

WILLIAM HOWARD TAFT had been many things: Yalie, Bonesman, federal judge, solicitor general, secretary of war, governor of the Philippines, president of the United States of America. Through it all, his highest aspiration in life, to become chief justice of the Supreme Court, had eluded him. Another thing he'd never been—not that he'd ever truly wanted to—was a teetotaler.

That being said, he mused as he exerted every effort, both mental and physical, to avoid slipping off his barstool, *I don't think I've ever been drunker than I am right at this moment.*

"Hey, watch it," said Kowalczyk, elbowing Taft in the ribs—or, rather, at the padding surrounding them. He was completely turned around on his stool, engrossed in Rob's band as they set up their instruments on the tiny stage at the back of the bar. While guitars were unpacked and a drum kit assembled, Rob, still sloshed but sobered up enough to remain upright, walked to the center of the stage. It sagged visibly under the skinny man's weight.

"I can't remember the last time I saw a punk show," Kowalczyk said, swaying a bit in his seat. "I guess if you're gonna ring in the New Year, you might as well do it loud." He pivoted around and yelled at Sam, "Hey, is your brother's band any damn good?"

From behind the bar, Sam snorted. "No. They're terrible." She plucked a mug from a bin of dirty water and began drying it with an equally dirty rag. "That's the whole point."

"I'm afraid I don't understand," Taft said, assembling the sentence using the full focus of his concentration.

"It's hard to explain," said Kowalczyk. "Let's just say that punk rock isn't trying to be pretty. It's . . . it's kind of like protest music."

"Protesting what?" spit Taft.

"Intelligence, mostly," cut in Sam. "At least in the Lousy Kissers' case. Don't get me wrong. I'm more of a classic-rock girl myself, but I've got nothing against punk. Honestly, though, Rob's band makes GG Allin look like Beethoven."

To punctuate her point, the haggard guitarist of the Lousy Kissers let loose an exploratory stab of feedback from his amplifier. Taft picked up two napkins and used them to cover his ears. "Isn't it a little early for them to be starting?" he yelled over the din. "I thought this was meant to be the evening's entertainment. For lack of a better word."

"Uh, Bill," said Sam, slipping two more shots of bourbon across the bar to Taft and Kowalczyk as if performing a magic trick, "it *is* evening. It's nine-thirty."

"Nine-thirty?" He rooted around his body for a pocket watch, then remembered he no longer carried one. No one did. He sighed, took out his phone, and hastily thumbed past a few missed calls from Susan and Rachel to check the time. "Thunderation." She was right. The last few hours had slipped by in a watery, whiskey-drenched haze.

Sam laughed and threw out her arms. "Welcome to my time machine."

Taft stared hard at her. "Oh, don't even get me started about time machines, young lady."

Kowalczyk jabbed him in the ribs again. Rather than looking suspicious, though, Sam flashed Taft a dazzling smile. "Young lady! It's been a long time since someone called me that. Let alone a distinguished gentleman like yourself."

It may have been the booze, but Taft could have sworn he heard a note of something other than teasing in Sam's tone. It had been a long time—longer than he cared to remember, seeing as how a chill had crept into the conjugal bed soon after he and Nellie had married—since a woman had spoken to him in that way. Taft grabbed the shot of bourbon before him and downed it like a giant draining a thimble. "This is really doing wonders for me."

But neither Sam nor Kowalczyk heard him. Or anything else. At that moment, the Lousy Kissers started playing.

At first it was a dull roar. Then a sharp one. Then it sounded like a locomotive—no, a dozen locomotives, all crashing into one another. As if a switch had been thrown, the slouching, indolent-looking young men in the Lousy Kissers jumped to life. At the front was Rob, his body jerking in all directions like a puppet.

Puppets, however, didn't usually sound like they were dying.

"Good God. Is that boy in pain?" Taft yelled.

Sam rolled her eyes. "Only the existential kind."

The band played on. Taft couldn't tell one song from the next, but after a few minutes, his ears adjusted to the onslaught. He was able to discern a steady beat, a hint of a structure, and even the barest modicum of melody. What he couldn't decipher, though, was a single word Rob was screaming.

He turned to ask Kowalczyk for a translation, but the stool was empty. He looked up; Taft could see Kowalczyk's bald head among the crowd, bobbing in unison with a few other similarly shaved patrons.

"Forgive him," Taft said to Sam. "He's not acting his age. He's had a long few months."

"Oh, really? What did he do?"

"Well, he shot me, for one."

"And yet, here he his, drinking with you on New Year's Eve. That's quite a friend."

"He is, isn't he?"

"How about a lady friend? You got one of those?"

Taft thanked the heavens for the anesthetic effects of alcohol; for the first time since he'd awakened in this new century, the thought of Nellie didn't send a pang of agony through his soul. "No. None of those."

She laid a hand on his. Across her knuckles were tattooed the letters f-u-c-k. "You know something?" Her eyes bored into his as the Lousy Kissers reached a crescendo of cacophony. "You'd be damned handsome with some facial hair. You ever thought about growing a mustache?"

TAFT WOKE UP the next morning, the first day of the year 2012, with a magnificent headache, no memory of the previous few hours, and a snoring, nude woman on top of him.

Upon waking a moment later, Sam seemed as startled as he was. Then she kissed him and laid her head back down his chest. "Happy new year, Bill. Way to ring it in, huh?"

Half an hour later, both of them panting and tangled in sheets, she finally relinquished her perch and rolled over on the bed next to him.

"Sam, I don't know what to—".

"Nothing. That's exactly what you should say. Just shut up and bask. I *know* that you know how good that was."

"Are all women of the twenty-first century as . . . robust as you?"

She laughed. "Twenty-first century? You really weren't kidding about that time-machine business last night, were you?"

Taft lifted his head. A wave of nausea washed over him. "Where's Kowalczyk?" he asked, as concerned about his friend as he was anxious to change the subject.

"Don't worry. He's on the couch. It's funny, no matter how drunk he got last night, he wouldn't let you out of his sight. When he insisted on coming back here with us, I was afraid he was talking about a threesome." She grinned mischievously. "Well, not *afraid*, exactly. But he passed out in the living room as soon as we got here."

She reached over and ran a finger across his cheek. "It's funny. He acts less like your buddy and more like your bodyguard. I wonder why that is?"

"He is, ah, very loyal."

Sam got on her knees in the bed and drew herself up, shoulders back. Scars and a hint of wrinkles were mixed in with the faded tattoos. This was a woman who had clearly seen more than her fair share of hard times. Yet, he had to admit, there was a wild, raw beauty to her. Not to mention an uneven smile that seemed suddenly slightly deranged.

"Oh, come on, Bill. I know who you are. Known all along. You don't live through all the things I have without being a suspicious bitch. You're Taft." With that, she moved over to straddle his legs, effectively pinning him to the mattress. With panic twining around the uneasiness in his gut, he glanced out the slightly ajar door to see Kowalczyk's stockinged feet sticking up over the arm of a sofa.

"Me? Taft? Nonsense. I mean, who's Taft?"

Sam licked her lips. "You know, I've never slept with a president before. Fuck, I've never even voted." She threw her head back and started cackling madly. Then, as abruptly as she started, she leaned forward and held down his arms. Her dirty blond hair tickled his face; her breath was sweetly, sourly enticing.

"Are you ready for round two, Mr. President?" Her tongue darted out and ran across the place where his mustache used to be. "This one's going to be even better. My husband should be home in about twenty minutes. How about you and I take a quick dip in the shower, then surprise him with a three-way?"

Within the span of ten seconds, Sam was on the floor, an ear-piercing alarm was shrieking like a banshee, Taft had yanked the befuddled Kowalczyk up from the couch, and the two were running out the door of Sam's house toward their rental car.

CLASSIFIED
Secret Service Incidence Report
BBR20120101.01
Agent Ira Kowalczyk

Please disregard use of the panic button. Big Boy activated the alert accidentally. There is no security emergency. Will review panic button procedures.

TWENTY

WITHIN A QUARTER of an hour, Kowalczyk had threaded their way out of Sam's rundown suburb and onto the highway. They both exhaled in relief as the odometer launched up to sixty. Other than that, they didn't make a sound.

After a Herculean struggle to dress his voluminous frame while sitting, Taft leaned his head against the cool glass of the window and let his thoughts drift. What had he been thinking? Granted, New Year's Eve was the most appropriate time to act inappropriately. But last night's behavior wasn't in his character. Or perhaps it was; as flabbergasted and deeply mortified at his own reckless actions as he was, he felt an odd glow of—dare he think it—pride. He'd spent so much of his life trying to appease others. Appearing sober, genial, and respectable at all times was the first step at accomplishing that. And yet, as he'd learned so many times during his first life, trying to make everyone happy inevitably made them all howl for your blood. Yes, he'd been selfish last night—selfish, impulsive, and utterly oblivious to what others thought of him. But damned if it hadn't felt good.

Strangely, though, as Taft's thoughts wandered through a foggy, disconnected fugue of feelings and memories, one thing kept recurring: Susan. He'd spent two months in the near-daily company of a learned, compassionate, scholarly woman whose primary interest in life was, well, *him*. She was, frankly, the kind of woman to whom he'd always been drawn, but he could not have been less interested. And yet now he'd jumped in bed with the first floozy who'd gotten him drunk. His queasiness returned with a vengeance.

"Kowalczyk. Pull over. Now."

Kowalczyk flashed him a livid scowl for breaking their silence, but his look softened as soon as he saw Taft's face. A moment later, Taft let loose a geyser of vomit across the dashboard. Keeping cool, Kowalczyk edged the car to the side of the highway. As soon as the tires noisily hit the coarse asphalt of the shoulder, Taft had already flung open his door; by the time Kowalczyk pulled to a full stop, Taft had emptied the steaming contents of his stomach into the cold air.

"What," gasped Taft, "did I eat last night?"

"Do you really want me to answer that question?" said Kowalczyk, wrinkling his nose.

Taft shot him the most offended look he could muster. "I'm serious. I don't remember anything past the popcorn."

"Bill, that Rob kid ran next door to Herbert's and brought back a friggin' wheelbarrow full of that shitty food. Hot dogs, nacho fries, Bombers. You must have sucked down your own weight in that sludge, and then some."

Taft gaped at him and then hung his head out the open door and vomited some more. As his insides knotted up and his eyes filled with tears, he could think of only one thing: to thank all that was holy that Susan couldn't see him right now. Or Irene, or Rachel, or Trevor. But especially Abby. Dear, sweet, angelic little Abby.

Wiping his mouth, he reached around to the back seat and into his open suitcase. He rummaged around for a moment and pulled out the good-luck charm Abby had smuggled into it. The Taft action figure. It was already grossly inaccurate; if the toy were large as life and made of flesh, it would weigh a good 75 pounds less than he did at the moment. But it was unrecognizable in another way. The look on its little face was friendly, crinkly-eyed, happy.

The little fellow also had a mustache. A grand, manly, granite-colored mustache.

A presidential-looking mustache.

Taft pulled out his phone. He was about to call Rachel, but he realized there were five more messages from Susan since he'd checked his phone at the bar the day before. He got out of the car, walked a few yards into the brown grass along the highway, and hit the key that dialed Susan's number. She answered almost before the first ring sounded.

"Bill? Oh, God, Bill. Look, I'm sorry I've been calling so much. This is big, though. Really big."

"Susan. Slow down, if you please. What's going on?"

He heard her take a deep breath. "Bill, they're trying to get you on the ballot."

"Who?"

"Who do you think? The Tafties. God, I hate that word. I mean, the Taft Party. Them and that kook Allen the Electrician. Not to mention our pal Pauline Craig. They've mobilized. They're pushing to get you put on the ballot in all fifty states. As a third-party candidate. As the head of the Taft Party. Or, failing that, they say they'll settle for telling the whole nation to vote for you as a write-in candidate."

"When did this happen?"

"They announced it yesterday. Press conference, media blitz, the works—my God, you really haven't been watching the news, have you?"

Taft made a small, noncommittal noise.

"But, Bill, there's something else. Something even scarier."

He was almost afraid to ask. "Yes? Out with it."

"The polls. They're going crazy. I know this is the most horrifying thing you could possibly imagine right now, but the polls are overwhelmingly in your favor. Not just to get on the ballot—to be a *competitive candidate*. Of course, the Republicans are still all shaking themselves out, but no matter which of those jokers they match you against—you know, Governor Rockstar, Governor Frownyface, Senator Wackadoodle—you're still holding your own against them, and you're not all that far behind the president. Bill, somehow you've *connected*. America wants you to run. And if these numbers are to be believed, they want you back. In the White House."

Taft stood there, blinking. The wind—blowing up from the prairie, perhaps across half the continent or more—poured over him. Above him, the vast American sky stretched like a vaulted ceiling from horizon to horizon. He thought of all the great and bizarre and horrifying things he'd seen and learned about this new United States, but also about how, underneath it all, it was still the country he knew and loved. He felt a sudden chill right down to his bones.

"Bill? Are you there? Bill?" Susan's voice squawked from the phone.

"Susan. I'm here. I mean to say, I'm *really* here. I'm coming."

"What? Bill, what do you mean?"

"I'm coming back, Susan. Hold tight, will you? And get ready. I'm coming back."

PART II
2012

"Don't sit up nights thinking about making me president, for that will never come, and I have no ambition in that direction. Any party which would nominate me would make a great mistake."

—William Howard Taft, while serving as governor of the Philippines under President Theodore Roosevelt, 1903

I SAW TAFT! (Penn Quarter)
Date: 2012-01-03 4:25PM EST

William Howard Taft was walking around the District today! I almost didn't recognize him; he's taken a razor to his 'stache, so now he looks less like Santa Claus and more like John Goodman.

I was thinking about it. You know how the world seems to have gone utterly batshit crazy in the past ten years? We've had terrorists smashing planes into our cities, we've had the U.S. armed forces in Iraq forever now, we've had all these tsunamis and hurricanes and crackdowns in the Middle East and all this horrible, horrible shit. But then now—now there's this guy, back to life, out of nowhere, and he's a good guy. You can just tell. Maybe . . . I dunno, maybe it's finally a bit of good crazy, to kind of start offsetting the bad crazy. Just a little. Just enough to let us know that it's not all for shit.

Or maybe I'm drunk. Before 5 p.m., even.

• Location: Penn Quarter

FROM THE DESK OF REP. RACHEL TAFT
(Ind.–OH)

Notes—Tues. 3rd—Do I really want to run for vice president?

Cons:

—We won't win. Third parties don't. Lot of time and ulcers to put into losing.

—Distraction from legislation, just when it's time to introduce the International Foods Act.

—Crass exploitation of family name instead of personal achievements.

—Putting Abby and Trevor through the ringer.

—Putting stress on relationship with Grandpa.

—Putting stress on Grandpa, period. How can this be a good idea for him?

Pros:

—We won't win. Ought to make it easy to stay honest.

—None of the other challengers are much to write home about anyway.

—Populist celebrity means influence means my legislation gets more support. Sometimes. Maybe.

—Crass exploitation of family name has worked very well for Kennedys, Bushes, etc.

—Trevor and Abby think we should do it.

—Well, why DID Wm Howard get zapped into the future, if not for this?

From _Taft: A Tremendous Man_, by Susan Weschler:

When I went to work for President Taft as his liaison to the twenty-first century, the first order of business was to start him off with a basic primer on the most important events that had happened in America and the world since he'd vanished. He dove right into the big-scale history and ate it right up. But when it came to the personal history, to the question of how his own disappearance had directly affected his own familiar world, it was a different story. He didn't want to hear about it. He wasn't ready to process it.

When he returned to Washington, D.C., after his New Year's road trip, there was a new resolve in his eyes. He asked me if he could look at that folder, the one he'd shied away from two months earlier. I gave it to him, and I will never forget the look in his eyes as he opened it to find, sitting on top, a black and white photograph. I knew what he was seeing: his wife. His beloved Nellie and all his children, along with the rest of his family, his friends, his colleagues. They stood outdoors, in a familiar place: Arlington National Cemetery.

"That's . . . that's my grave, isn't it? That's a photograph of my funeral." It wasn't a question. It was obvious.

I told him: After he'd gone missing from Wilson's inauguration, there'd been a citywide search. Then nationwide. Then worldwide. After months, it was clear he wasn't to be found. Theories abounded. Had he been kidnapped by a foreign power? Did he run away from the pressures of politics to live a quiet life incognito? Was it suicide? But eventually it was clear that the nation needed a funeral. So an empty casket was buried at Arlington. He was the first president to be buried in the national military cemetery, though of course no part of his body actually lay there.

Tears were rolling down President Taft's cheeks as he saw this picture of his own memorial, this tableau that no man ever sees. Then I saw his face harden as his eyes flickered from the image of his wife and children to the man standing next to them. Teddy Roosevelt. The man who'd been his friend. The man who'd then spent Taft's last two years relentlessly tearing him down in public, trying to reclaim the office he'd previously seemed glad to hand off to his friend. There stood Roosevelt at Taft's funeral, a hand of comfort on Nellie's shoulder. I could only imagine what was going through his mind.

"President Taft," I said, "Roosevelt delivered a eulogy for you. I think you might be interested to read it."

"No," he said. "No, Miss Weschler, I would not be so interested." He closed the folder and shook his head. "It's done. It's the past. It's gone. Let us look to the future."

TWENTY-ONE

THE FRAYED DENIM and faded flannel of Allen "the Electrician" Holtz's clothes—the same ones he always seemed to wear—carried a calming, workaday aura. Taft found himself staring down at the man's attire, avoiding his eyes, as Allen escorted him, with Susan at his side, into the living room of the modest suburban D.C. home that had been chosen for their meeting. "A little summit or something," a laughing Allen had assured Taft over the phone. "But, seriously, nothing fancy."

Taft apparently had a different idea of fanciness, or the lack thereof, than Allen did. The large living room was packed from wall to wall with people. They sat and stood and even crouched in silence, each of them staring at Taft with a frozen expression of slack-jawed awe.

Then the room erupted.

"Taft!"

"Mr. President!"

"Oh my God, I can't believe it's him! I can't believe it's you!"

The miniature mob moved in, babbling with excitement. His shoulders were patted. A comely middle-aged woman in a "Draft Taft!" T-shirt stole a kiss from his cheek. Clammy palms were pressed into his own limp hand, which was too shocked to shake back.

Within seconds Taft's muscle memory took over. He smiled that empty yet enthusiastic campaign-trail smile perfected in railcar restrooms and hotel mirrors across the continent a hundred years ago. He returned greetings and humbly parried compliments with the ease of an automaton. Several times, his eyes flicked over to the chair where Allen sat; the man's face hovered halfway between smirking mischief and beaming pride.

"Okay, everyone, let's give Mr. Taft some room to breathe here!" Allen got to his feet, raised his voice and hands, and quieted the crowd. "Maybe some kind soul would like to offer the man a seat?"

A loveseat immediately presented itself. Taft offered Susan a cushion, then sank down beside her. Before he'd even settled, a tray of Fulsom PizzaBombs—still in the soggy cardboard box, presumably straight out of the microwave—was shoved under his nose.

"Uh, no, thank you," he said, waving away the tray and accepting instead a bottle of water. Already sweating due to the surprise as well as the press of bodies in the room, he took a swig— and almost spit the liquid right back out as his tongue registered a strange flavor that had no business being present. He looked at the label on the bottle: MapleWater. Truly, he thought, did the people of this age really feel it necessary to try to improve upon *water*?

"Everybody refreshed, then?" Allen strode to the center of the room. "Let's talk Taft."

"So, Mr. Holtz," Taft said. "You and your associates in this Taft Party would have me run for president once again. What do you envision?"

"Mr. Taft," said Allen, "we want to give the American people a voice to say their piece. Because God knows they don't get to have a say with the Ds and the Rs, the way things are now."

Taft nodded warily. "I follow you, sir."

"The Taft Party: now there's something the players will have to listen to, right? You're a big man. I mean, not that you're a big man, but, you know what I mean."

"Indeed."

"So we've been talking about a hard-hitting campaign. We'd call it the Blunt Truth campaign; we'll be all about telling it like it is. We'll start right off, hitting the president where he's weakest—"

"No."

Allen blinked. "Uh, sorry?"

"Mr. Holtz, everyone, I must make this perfectly clear. Rachel and I will run under the Taft Party banner; it seems we would be foolish to let our name march on without us, just as it would be foolish for you to try! But I have been through this wringer twice before, and we shall do it my way. And that means, first and foremost, we are not running to bring down the politicians. They can do that perfectly well themselves. No. We are running to lift up the people. We're here to establish the Taft Party as a veritable bastion of reason and fairness in political life, because Lord knows such a bastion is needed. We're here, as you say, to provide a voice for the good women and men of America who can't be heard over the din of all this twenty-first-century madness. And we are here to run the sort of campaign I have always believed in: an honest test of thoughtful discourse."

"Uh," said Allen. "Mr. Taft, I'm probably not the person to be telling you this." His gaze slid to Susan and back again. "But things aren't as cut and dried as they were back in your day. The world's a complicated place. It ain't as black and white as all that."

Taft wished his mustache were there to hide his sudden snarl. "You think, sir, that things were black and white in my day?" Allen looked startled. "I assure you, that was just the photography. My presidency had *every* motive and opportunity to overstep its political and moral bounds, both here and abroad. I made some decisions that I know were wrong. I made far more that may have made my job harder, and may have asked for more of a sacrifice from the country, but they were simply the right and decent things to do. Don't patronize or preach to *me*. I don't care if you're from the year 20,000. I've still seen more of the grays of this world than you ever will. The only difference is, I don't cloak myself in them. No, sir. If you want me as your candidate, Mr. Holtz, you shall have to allow me to run my own campaign."

The man stuck out his hand. "Sounds like a deal." They shook on it, and although Allen's wiry hand was engulfed in Taft's thick one, the man cocked an eyebrow. "But . . . you'll let us suggest practical details, right?"

"Certainly, certainly," Taft said. "What did you have in mind?"

"Well, Mr. Taft, see, I was thinking about your announce-ment . . ."

TWITTER—Jan. 17, 2012

taft2012
No sooner have I grown accustomed to the wonders of Google, I am introduced to the wizardry of Twitter! So, this is the new town square. Gree

taft2012
Well do I recall the wave of excitement that flooded the world upon the introduction of the telephone. So it surprises me not a bit that Twi

taft2012
It appears I have misunderstood the functioning of this 140-letter transmission. My apologies, readers, for the confusion! I have the hang o

taft2012
Aha. The blank spaces are to be counted as well.

taft2012
How remarkable. It is true what they say: It is harder to speak in few words than in many.

taft2012
Well, of one thing you may be assured from these awkward rhetorical fumblings: It is I, William Howard Taft, behind this faceless broadcast.

jamesjamesjames
Wait, hang on, @taft2012 is really Taft? #Taft

Robbrenner

@jamesjamesjames I think @taft2012 is just that same roleplayer who's been doing shtick since the *President Kane* Blu-Ray came out. #Taft

njerica

@Robbrenner Hang on, @taft2012 keeps getting retweeted by @TaftPartyUSA—that might really be him! #Taft

TaftPartyUSA

To answer all the questions, yes, @taft2012 is the big man himself! Everyone follow him—there's an announcement coming! #Taft

tunabubbles

@TaftPartyUSA Hope he's going to announce that he finally knows how to count to 140. #Taft #Fail #TaftFail

njerica

An announcement coming from @taft2012 via @TaftPartyUSA? OMG, I don't believe it . . . #Taft

Robbrenner

LOL @tunabubbles, he's going to announce that he's all washed up now, but he could really use a hand getting dry. #TaftFail

taft2012

I, William Howard Taft, am honored and humbled to answer the Taft Party's call to stand in the 2012 presidential election.

taft2012

I am further honored to have Congresswoman Rachel Taft—a strong, brilliant, devoted Ohioan and American if I do say so—as my running mate.

njerica

Holy crap, it's for real! #Taft #2012election

JudgeMatthews

@taft2012 This is amazing. Finally, we're going to have a candidate with the right experience to be president. He's BEEN president.

njerica

Will never forget where I was when I saw @taft2012 on TV the 1st time. Now know what old folks mean when they say that about the Challenger.

jamesjamesjames

@taft2012 @TaftPartyUSA Where do I sign up as a campaign volunteer? #Taft

SamFromChicago666

@jamesjamesjames You and me both. That man is hot stuff. About time the Oval Office held some real beefcake! #Taft

FollowTheLogicChain

@jamesjamesjames Volunteer? Don't. It's all bullshit. You really believe President Taft came back like King Arthur to lead us? #TaftIsAHoax

jamesjamesjames

@FollowTheLogicChain Jeez, you hoaxers really believe the govt would make UP something this insane? Sometimes reality's weird but awesome.

FollowTheLogicChain

@jamesjamesjames Believe in your version of reality if you will. I prefer actual reality. #TaftIsAHoax

LindaBeach

@jamesjamesjames There's a volunteer forum at taft2012.com! Come join us. #Taft #2012election

IanTheArtist

@SamFromChicago666 Did you know Taft was the president who had the Oval Office built in the first place? #Taft

SamFromChicago666

@IanTheArtist I did not know that.

"The president can exercise no power which cannot be fairly and reasonably traced to some specific grant of power in the Constitution or in an act of Congress. There is no vague extra power which he can exercise because it seems to him to be in the public interest."

—*William Howard Taft, speech to the Delaware Taft Party, Feb. 22, 2012*

"Substantial progress toward better things can rarely be taken without developing new evils requiring new remedies. Look at modern agriculture—companies like Fulsom have delivered affordable foodstuffs in huge quantities that can feed Americans bountifully no matter their income, yet the food is not good; it makes me queasy both digestively and morally."

—*William Howard Taft, speech to the West Virginia Taft Party, Feb. 25, 2012*

"I am in favor of helping the prosperity of all countries because, when we are all prosperous, the trade with each becomes more valuable to the other."

—*William Howard Taft, speech to the Kansas Taft Party, March 2, 2012*

"Don't worry over what the newspapers say. I don't; why should anyone else?"

—*William Howard Taft, speech to the Wyoming Taft Party, March 5, 2012*

PAULINE CRAIG: Welcome to *Raw Talk*. I'm Pauline Craig, and today I'll be talking with some outspoken supporters of William Howard Taft's historic reentry into presidential politics. Joining me first via satellite is Frank Lommel, former president of the United Food and Factory Workers Local 15 in Colorado and now the Midwest coordinator for the Taft Party USA. Mr. Lommel, tell us how your friends in the union have responded to the Taft Party throwing its hat into the ring for the 2012 election.

FRANK LOMMEL: Hi, Pauline, thanks for having me. Obviously, I don't speak for the Local 15 anymore, but I've heard from a lot of workers who say they're awfully interested in the Taft Party. They understand how abso-friggin' great it is that a candidate who's got such an incredible record of going after big, monopolistic businesses is being taken seriously by voters all across the country.

PAULINE CRAIG: Let's talk about that. When President Taft was in the White House a hundred years ago, breaking up monopolies—busting trusts, as they called it then—was his number-one priority. But is that really the issue that faces the workforce today? Health-care costs, huge unemployment rates, no respect from the liberal elite for enrolling students in good, solid vocational training—aren't those the workforce problems any president will have to deal with?

FRANK LOMMEL: Pauline, it all comes back to giant conglomerates that think they can act any darn way they please. If you look at the meat-processing industry, for instance, you see that there are huge numbers of low-paid immigrant workers being employed in the slaughterhouses and rendering facilities who haven't had the freedom to unionize because *all* the big protein companies are specifically looking to keep wages low across the board. It's not like these poor guys can go across the street and apply for a job at a more enlightened poultry producer. So the companies are collectively engaged in the sorts of behavior that monopolies can get away with, even though they're not technically monopolies. That's the sort of thing we Tafties know that William Howard Taft would never stand for—not a guy who's proven himself willing to tackle the toughest conglomerates in the nation.

PAULINE CRAIG: Big Labor. A demographic that always votes Democrat. And Frank Lommel is here on *Raw Talk* to say that a 155-year-old Republican-turned-third-party independent has at least one ex-union leader's support. That's something you don't see every day.

TWENTY-TWO

ALBUQUERQUE LOOKED LIKE just another twinkling grid riveted into the landscape, one of dozens Taft had seen from his airplane window over the past several weeks as he'd begun to reacquaint himself with the now much quicker paced business of campaigning. Now that he'd become accustomed—or at least numb—to air travel, the whole business of looking down on the world from a six-mile height didn't seem so unnatural. He'd even been able to enjoy and keep down a few dozen packets of delicious sweet nuts he'd been given by the fetching brunette attendant. They paired quite well, he had to admit, with the tiny bottles of whiskey he'd been steadily consuming since takeoff.

Taft licked the astringent sweetness from the tips of his fledgling whiskers and sighed.

"What's the matter? You're not getting sick again, are you?" Kowalczyk was staring at him and misinterpreting his downcast expression. The agent rooted around in the pocket on the back of the seat in front of him and drew out a paper sack.

"What did you call that again?" Taft asked as Kowalczyk popped the sack open.

"Barf bag."

"Ah, yes. Barf bag. The eloquence of the twenty-first century never ceases to astound me. See, Kowalczyk? This is why I need you to accompany me on my travels. How could I possibly survive in this dazzling new world without knowing the proper nomenclature of the barf bag?"

Kowalczyk made a face at him. "Someone has to teach you the basics of survival while Professor Weschler is teaching you all the complicated stuff."

Taft looked around to make sure Susan hadn't returned to her seat yet—how could anyone, no matter their size, squeeze into those infernally small airplane bathrooms, anyway?—and leaned his forehead against the cold pane of the window. "Susan is a dear woman, a learned scholar, and, all in all, a good friend. But I must say . . . I cannot quite forget that she jots down all that I do and it will end up in a book eventually." Kowalczyk smiled faintly, and suddenly Taft felt a chill run through his body. "Kowalczyk. You aren't going to write a book about me, are you?"

The agent snorted. "I ought to say yes—that's what you get for insisting your Secret Service agent do double duty as your confidante. No, Mr. President, sir, I intend to devote all my attention to guarding your ass for a long time to come. I'll let other people worry about analyzing it."

When they landed, Rachel was there to meet them, a staff aide in tow. They drove to a nearby diner, one of these gleaming fortresses of greasiness that calls itself Denny's, and, as Taft squeezed through the narrow aisles between tables, he saw Trevor and Abby waiting for them at a large booth. His heart leapt at the sight of his great-great-granddaughter; this would be her one visit to the campaign trail, since her parents were determined to preserve her normal life at home with her father as much as possible while Rachel split the season between stumping with Taft and fulfilling her legislative duties on Capitol Hill.

With a prudence he was proud to muster, Taft poured himself a cup of coffee from the pot on the table and gulped it down before wedging himself into the booth—a laborious process that, he noticed with a scowl, amused the nearby tables to no end. "Damned shoddy construction," he muttered, then poured himself another cup of coffee. He could already feel himself sobering up. Oh, Nellie would have had a mouthful to say about his occasional nip at the bottle. Prohibition was nothing but a dim, distant memory to this nation—although, Taft had to admit, what he'd seen of the country's current legislation against recreational pharmaceuticals was no less misguided and ineffectual. He turned to Abby, hoping the coffee had sufficiently masked the booze on his breath.

"So, what's new with you, young lady?"

She stared at him sternly. "Grandpa, you got bigger."

"Ah, well, yes. More of me to love and all that, wouldn't you say? Speaking of which, unless I'm mistaken, you've gotten taller."

"How can you tell? I'm sitting down."

"Your daughter doesn't miss a thing, does she?" he said to Trevor.

Trevor smiled. "Well, she is a Collins. And a Taft."

Just then, the waitress came by with a handful of massive menus. Taft opened his and stared at the glorious selection of savory riches detailed therein.

All in all, Taft decided, the twin thrills of whiskey and coffee stimulating his blood, this trip was starting out swimmingly.

TWENTY-THREE

THE RALLIES IN DELAWARE and West Virginia had been warm-ups. The ones in Kansas and Wyoming had been surprisingly comfortable. And now, as he stood on the raised platform in the middle of this weathered county fairground and waved happily to satisfying applause from the fine people of Albuquerque, New Mexico, Taft felt a surge of the grudging, nervous excitement that he'd first experienced while stumping in 1908. He glanced to his left, where Rachel sat beaming; she was feeling it, too.

"As you can see," he said, his voice booming through the speakers as he gestured to the huge red, white, and blue banners that hung behind him, "great effort has been taken to today to make me appear presidential." A good-hearted laugh ran through the crowd. "Suffice it to say, I never have. But I take that as a good thing." He paused for a moment as if expecting to be challenged, but the only sound he could hear was the wind whistling through the nearby trees. "America, and please correct me if I'm wrong, is a democracy, which is much more than a mere political apparatus. At its core, it was intended to be the triumph, the apotheosis, of the people. No despots or tyrants or plutocrats, but people." A light smattering of applause filled the silence as Taft squared his shoulders. "But I'm not here to reaffirm some image of myself as a common man. Clearly, I am no such thing. In fact, unlike so many of my opponents on both sides of the big-ticket coin, I'm not here to talk about myself at all. I'm here to talk about you.

"You are America. You are a piece of it, and you are the whole of it. And so is your neighbor. Whoever stands next to you is a part of your existence, as is the person who stands halfway across the country. No part of this country works properly if any part of it is failing, just as no body is healthy if even the smallest cell of it is ill. An entire symphony becomes discordant at the creation of one wrong note. And my opponents have been blowing quite a few of them lately."

The crowd seemed to stir, forgoing a laugh at Taft's obvious punch line in anticipation of his point. They were here to witness a spectacle, a happening, a moment—and, by God, he'd give them one.

"And just as no man, woman, or child in this country is truly healthy if his neighbor is not, so it goes with two of mankind's most basic needs: sustenance and education. Trust me, I am well acquainted with both. And I also know, in the essential matters of food and schools, that quantity and quality are not interchangeable. What's that saying you have these days? 'Garbage in, garbage out'? For too long, I have come to understand, America has been content to let those in power—the would-be dictators of both the public and private sectors—feed you garbage. This garbage is presented in many forms: lower wages for public school teachers. Political and corporate pressures on curricula. Reckless agribusiness. Relaxed standards and regulations of the food industry. And then there's the intersection of the two problems: the toxic crossroads we call student lunch. It may seem a small thing, granted, in the grand scheme of this vast nation. But if you want to look at one of the major roots of the lack of self-reliance and the lack of self-regard in this country, look no further. Again, I speak from experience. And if elected, I will not allow such circumstance to stand. It is long past time for the Department of Education to be recognized as one of the most important entities in the entire federal government!"

Taft paused to allow the crowd a chance to respond. He was greeted with a shuffling of feet. A phone rang. Some pro-Taft signs previously held highly and proudly seemed to dip and wobble with indecision.

Time seemed to crawl. He'd known this was going to be a hard sell in an America obsessed with terrorism and rampant unemployment and partisan squabbles, but he had to play his own game. Or rather: he had to play no game at all.

A hand shot up in the third row, and Taft gestured magnanimously in its direction. It was a man—a fat man of perhaps forty, Taft saw, as round as himself though certainly not as tall, wearing thick eyeglasses and sporting an unshaven face.

"So, Mr. Taft," the man sneered. "You say that the Department of Education holds the key to America's future. But there was no such department in the presidential cabinet when you were alive, was there, Mr. Taft? Why should you place such weight on a bureaucracy you couldn't possibly know anything about?"

Ah. A heckler. One of those malcontents who'd already decided to shout without listening in return. Taft knew the type well, and they made him cringe. Even when he held the highest office in the land, he'd always striven to appease both sides of any conflict, to compromise and find equitable resolution wherever possible. After all, it appealed to his sense of justice and fairness, the same sense that, early in his career, had led him toward becoming a judge. More than that, though, he'd always been sensitive to the sting of scorn, no matter how slight or even imagined; he always felt guilty when confronted by one of these closed-minded mockers, for surely their misunderstanding arose from his own failure to explain himself successfully. Nellie used to scold him for it. She assumed being president would grow him a thicker hide. He patted his gut, all those extra pounds he'd packed on since being elected, and again since awakening a hundred years later. He smiled sadly. A thicker hide, indeed.

"I say, sir, it is true that, in my day, the Office of Education was a minor entity in the Interior Department. But although its increased size today doubtless holds some inefficiencies, I find no fault with its enlarged mandate to help educate America's children. How can we face the future, sir, without teaching our young people all they can possibly know?" He turned to call upon another raised hand, but the fat man shouted back at him.

"You're full of shit! You don't sound like William Howard Taft! You aren't William Howard Taft! You're a freaking hoax, and everyone with a brain has got to know it!" His eyes wild, the man suddenly leveled a large, black pistol in Taft's direction.

Then several things happened at once.

As Taft, his imagination long sharpened by the keen awareness that both McKinley and Roosevelt had faced bullets from their constituents, hurled himself sideways to shield Rachel from harm, she did the exact same thing, and the two of them crashed into each other and fell to the stage while, Taft saw out of the corner of his eye, Kowalczyk went flying through the air, over the heads of the first two rows of the crowd, and tackled the fat man in a messy heap.

"Are you all right?" Rachel yelled.

"Unharmed," Taft coughed.

"Stay down," she said. As people swarmed around them, they

turned to look toward the scuffle.

Kowalczyk stood up, the man's gun in his hand and the man under the agent's foot. "It's not real," he shouted. "It's a toy gun. It's a fake."

The fat man began cackling. "It's as real as he is!" he shouted, pointing at Taft. "It's every bit as real as he is!"

TWENTY-FOUR

TAFT CLOSED HIS EYES to shut out the sight of Kowalczyk pacing furiously around their hotel suite. The man was barking instructions into his service radio, and it was giving Taft a headache. Slowly, however, he became aware that his bodyguard was calling for a larger contingent of agents to be dispatched to the campaign, and Taft stood up and motioned furiously for silence. Kowalczyk finished the call and drilled his eyes into Taft's. "What's wrong?"

"Please, Kowalczyk. No additional security! I know fretting about it is your job, but I'm already trapped in this entire century I never asked for. I don't need the walls around me to be even tighter than they have been!"

"Bill. Mr. President, sir. We can't keep allowing you to be so vulnerable. I already can't believe I went along with your crazy two-man vacation thing, and that nothing worse happened then. Today was a long overdue wake-up call."

"Nonsense! And what matter if I *had* been shot, I ask you. I'm living a charmed second life already. Every day is gravy."

"Are you nuts? That's exactly why we can't let anything happen to you!" The agent stumbled over his words. "I mean, you know, on top of the fact that you're our friend, Bill. You're—you're a one of a kind miracle. We can't have William Howard Taft magically come back to life and just let him get killed again!"

"Anachronism or not, Kowalczyk, time traveler or not, I am indeed just another man. And don't forget, I used to travel the country extensively while I was president. And not just in the course of campaigning! I snuck out of the White House every chance I could get, and for as long as I could get away with."

"Yeah," Kowalczyk sighed, "you may have mentioned that a few dozen times while we were driving to Chicago. How in hell did you pull it off, anyway?"

"It was a different time then. We had the Secret Service, of course, but even with a recent assassination on our minds— McKinley—security was far less overweening than it is now. Perhaps it was the very fact that we hadn't yet invented all your new technological miracles, but it simply never occurred to us to even *try* to fortify every moment of our lives from harm. I'd accept invitations to anything and everything—commencement ceremonies, graduations, ribbon-cuttings, even the bar mitzvah of the son of an old colleague or college chum—just to get out of the that maddening, oppressive Oval Office." He chuckled. "And I'd take my sweet time getting there and returning. My critics called me a tramp, and I always chalked it up to wanderlust. In actuality, though, I was running away from that damnable cage."

"But didn't you get hassled constantly? Not just by random people, but by the press? I mean, we've had a recent president who spent way more time on vacation than he should have. But he was almost always hiding out at his ranch. The idea of a sitting president just up and roaming around America whenever he felt like it—it's just a logistical nightmare."

"That's the Secret Service man in you talking, not the Ira Kowalczyk who likes to flail his body around to the strains of banshees holding electrified guitars. Really, Kowalczyk, don't be paranoid."

The agent blinked at him. "You are saying that to a man who just tackled a loonie who could have been pointing a gun at you from the middle of a crowd. Hell, what am I even talking about—you're saying it to a man who *shot you myself* not six months ago, because you just suddenly turned up somewhere you had no business being."

Taft chuckled. "Yes, but neither of you actually meant to kill me, did you? Our friend today was merely making an ill-advised political statement with a child's toy—and you, sir, were defending your president! I dare say, that nick in my leg notwithstanding, I've been as safe with you by my side these past months as anyone possibly can be in the world. The world today, or the world a hundred years ago, or the world ever. It is an unsafe life, Kowalczyk. Every damn one of us—president, schoolgirl, ditch digger—we could all breathe our last at any time, and hiding from death does not a damn thing to alter that fact."

Kowalczyk was quiet a moment. "You really are a pretty remarkable guy, Bill."

"And you, my friend, have a remarkable flying tackle. Come— let me take you to dinner."

PAULINE CRAIG: And we're back with more *Raw Talk*. In the wake of Thursday's frightening threat on the life of Taft Party presidential candidate William Howard Taft, we're speaking with several members of the Taft Party to find out how, if at all, this changes the game for America's most unexpected dark-horse candidate. With me now via satellite is Professor Susan Weschler, chief aide to the candidate himself. Professor Weschler, first of all, let's begin with the important question: how is Mr. Taft doing? Surely he must be shaken up after his brush with violence.

SUSAN WESCHLER: Thank you, Pauline. You're right, that is the most important question. Mr. Taft is doing very well. As you know, while we had a scare for a moment there last week, there was no actual violence, and Mr. Taft and his campaign are rolling ahead as planned. We'll be holding Taft events tomorrow in Austin, Friday in Little Rock, and Tuesday in Miami.

PAULINE CRAIG: Jack Channing, the alleged assailant—according to the police, he's a classic fan turned-stalker case, a film buff who became obsessed with Orson Welles's *President Kane*, collected all sorts of memorabilia from the movie, and developed an unhealthy level of interest in President Taft's real life, to the point where his whole self-identity revolved around being the world's most knowledgeable Taft fan.

SUSAN WESCHLER: Uh, yes. That's, that's what they're saying. Again, we shouldn't forget that the man was harmless.

PAULINE CRAIG: Maybe harmless—definitely disturbing. Channing made a Web site way back in 1998 to present several elaborately spun theories as to what might have caused the president's disappearance in 1913. A freak horseback-riding accident on the bank of the Potomac River. Or an overblown conspiracy involving Taft's late father, Alphonso, who'd founded the secret Skull and Bones society at Yale. Channing was used to being the Taft guy with an answer to everything—so when the *real* Taft returned to life, they say Channing became obsessed with the idea that it had to be a hoax, because otherwise it would mean he didn't really know anything after all.

SUSAN WESCHLER: Well, I suppose that's the difference between a historian and a conspiracy nut. Those of us who really study history know that there's always the possibility of a new discovery that will throw everything we thought we knew into a whole new light. Whereas the conspiracy theorists are just practicing pseudo-history—they let their, uh, their personal, ah, feelings and beliefs about the subject matter become more important than pursuing the questions of actual historical truth.

PAULINE CRAIG: That's all well and good, Professor, but there are certainly a lot of regular Americans today whose feelings and beliefs about William Howard Taft have built his campaign into the historic phenomenon it is. Some of them are your colleagues in the Taft Party! Let's say hello to Matt Shelby, the Taft Party's Northwest regional coordinator. Matt, Bill Taft dodged an imaginary bullet last week. What about the metaphorical bullets? Some critics in the D.C. establishment have suggested that the Taft campaign doesn't have a cohesive political platform. How do you respond to that?

MATT SHELBY: Pauline, William Howard Taft's politics have been on record for a hundred years now. I'd have to say these critics are either too lazy to spend a few minutes looking them up, or they hold the

American people in such contempt that they think *they're* too lazy to look them up. Either way, they're wrong. President Taft governed in the twentieth century with the same principled convictions he'll govern with in the twenty-first. A determination to put the American people's interests first. A commitment to absolute honesty and accountability at every level of his administration. And an absolute respect for governing by the precise letter of the law.

PAULINE CRAIG: Victoria Freeman Eldridge, you've been responsible for the Taft Party's agenda in New England. While Matt Shelby here was a Democrat before he joined the Taft cause, you were a Republican.

VICTORIA FREEMAN ELDRIDGE: A Libertarian, actually, Pauline.

PAULINE CRAIG: But a fiscal conservative, for sure.

VICTORIA FREEMAN ELDRIDGE: Absolutely. I voted for Republican presidents most of my life because that was the closest I could get to a proper conservative candidate. That's why I was so excited to join the Taft Party—Taft doesn't just talk the conservative talk, he's the real deal. Under Taft, for instance, corporate taxes were the merest fraction of what they are now, and the economy flourished. American industry was booming back then, with new jobs being created every day by the thousands. We can have that kind of prosperity again, if we return to the simple, streamlined tax code that the first Taft administration put into place. I think it goes without saying that Taft is the man to do it.

SUSAN WESCHLER: Um—

PAULINE CRAIG: Just a moment, Professor Weschler. We'd like to say hello to the Reverend Todd Osborne, organizer of the Southern Taft Party organization.

REV. TODD OSBORNE: Thank you, Ms. Craig.

PAULINE CRAIG: Reverend Osborne, what does Taft mean to you?

REV. TODD OSBORNE: Well, now, I think we all recognize a good man when we see one. William Howard Taft was raised in a more decorous time, with a proper set of American values. We've all seen the culture in this nation fall to decadence and hedonism over the course of the past fifty years, and we all know the madness has got to stop if we don't want our children to be citizens of the United States of Amexico, working for poverty wages in call centers for Chinese and Indian corporations.

SUSAN WESCHLER: If I may—

REV. TODD OSBORNE: In Taft's day, Americans had pride and self-discipline—so much so that they banded together to form the great Prohibition movement and renounced self-indulgent living. Americans back then knew that having too much fun wasn't a good thing! I think we can look at the candidates in front of us today and know which of them stands for a responsible, upright, *moral* lifestyle.

PAULINE CRAIG: Professor Weschler, something to add?

SUSAN WESCHLER: Ah—I just—just that I hope the voters will come out and listen to Mr. Taft speak for himself in person. Or, um, online at taft2012—uh, on Twitter, Facebook, or dot-com.

PAULINE CRAIG: And we'll be back after this.

AUTHENTIC REPLICA—TAFT ASSAILANT'S FAKE PISTOL

Item condition: New

Quantity: 4 available

Time left: 2 days 15 hours

Buy It Now: U.S. $99.95

Description: For a limited time only! You can own this perfectly crafted reproduction of the toy pistol used by political protester Jack Channing to threaten former president William Howard Taft in Albuquerque on March 8, 2012. Painstaking review of news footage has shown the gun was produced by splicing together two production model toy weapons from Whimco, the RP-7 and the RPX-91. I have not only replicated this custom modification, but have also weathered the plastic casing identically to the markings that can be seen from every angle in the television coverage. Don't miss out on owning this practically unique piece of American history, a perfect reminder that Taft is the president who just cannot be kept down no matter what. Taft 2012!

LOCAL 12 WKRC-TV

The following message is paid for by the Friends of American Nutrition.

For ten years, Rachel Taft and her husband, trial lawyer Trevor Collins, filed lawsuit after lawsuit after lawsuit against hardworking farm owners throughout the Ohio countryside—just because they think farmers don't know the right way to raise food. Rachel Taft isn't a farmer—she's from downtown Cincinnati. And Trevor Collins isn't even from Ohio—he's from Detroit. What does an inner-city urban lawyer know about agriculture, anyway?

Now Rachel Taft is in Congress, trying to slap regulations on farmers all across the country. And we're supposed to believe that her running mate—her grandfather, William Howard Taft—is a "good old-fashioned real American"? Come on, Taft. Just because you were born a hundred fifty years ago doesn't mean we were born yesterday.

═══════════════════════

FROM THE DESK OF REP. RACHEL TAFT
(Ind.–OH)
Notes—Tues. 27th

—Oh, fuck you, Augustus Fulsom. "Inner-city urban lawyer." Fuck you in your turkey-mutilating ear.

March 20, 2012
Dear Mommy and Grandpa,

I am glad you are coming home soon! It's fun to see you on TV but I miss you anyway. Even though we talk on the phone before bed. Daddy is proud of you and says I should not listen to the angry farmer commercial and there's nothing bad about being from the city. He says that man is not a real farmer and that you only get mad at companies who make their farmers do gross things to the food.

I still want to bring Grandpa to show and tell!

Love,
Abby

P.S. Daddy showed me how to spell *commercial* and *companies*.

CLASSIFIED
Secret Service Incidence Report
BBR20120402.06
Agent Ira Kowalczyk

En route back to Ohio for week of speeches; have dispatched agents Pearsall and Horton to head advance sweep of venues in Cleveland, Columbus, Cincinnati. Note that Big Boy appears less concerned with security issues and more concerned about open access to chat with voters. Note also that Big Boy seems *most* concerned with making sure there's time to visit Irene Kaye in Patterson Senior Village. More security around the perimeter this time, since the crazies and hoaxers online are getting louder. (Site diagrams attached.)

TWENTY-FIVE

THE ROSEWATER SMELL had faded from Irene's room in the nursing home and been replaced by something saccharine and sickly chemical. She lay in bed when Taft arrived, various machines hooked into her body, her veins visible through her skin like blue pen through vellum. "It's about time," she rasped, a rattle at the edge of her voice. "I haven't got all day, you know. I might mean that quite literally."

Her laugh was weak, but there was no mockery to it. Even on her deathbed, Irene had more stoicism and spine than most of the twenty-first century combined.

"Irene." He took her fluttering hand. It felt as light as a parakeet. "I'm sorry I couldn't come sooner. Things have been . . . difficult these recent days."

"Difficult? Oh, Taft, don't let these times taint you. If there's one thing this generation loves, it's to make things more difficult than they have to be."

A blush rose to Taft's cheeks. He sighed and sat next to her on the bed.

"You've lost some paunch," she noted. "Last time you planted yourself there, I almost slid off and onto the floor."

Taft patted her hand. "Well, yes. I've been trying to take better care of myself."

"Ah," she said, "if only it were as easy as trying." She coughed violently, but it passed before Taft could ring the bell for the nurse. "It's all right," she assured him, although her tone was anything but. "They pop in every few minutes to check on me anyway. I believe they've got someone waiting out in the hallway, eager to take over my room the instant it becomes vacant."

"They may take your room, but no one will be able to take your place."

"You're a flatterer. And a maudlin one at that." She wheezed. "But please, tell me, what's on your mind? You seem twice as troubled as the last time you came to see me."

"Ah, well now, I. . . ." He cleared his throat. "Lord, Irene, this is hard to say. For as dedicated as I am to running this campaign fairly and honestly, I find that I'm still having to play these infuriating politician games. Again! I hated it in 1912, and it's even worse in 2012. It's not enough to be oneself. I start off trying to discuss the truth as I see it, but no matter how clear I try to be, people misunderstand something I say or they focus on one little thing that they don't like at the expense of the greater point I wish to make. And then, as I try to get closer to their perspective so that I might figure out how to explain what I want to say in words they'll grasp, what ends up happening is that I bend around, prevaricate, hedge, compromise, conceal. It's inhuman. I feel the rot of it taking hold of my soul."

"Oh, Bill. Don't be so melodramatic. Is it really that bad?"

Taft glanced around as if some partisan or spy was ready to eavesdrop or simply pounce on him. "It's these infernal Taft Party people. Not the voters—the tub-thumpers. They all think they can paint me as the champion of whatever sort of 'old-timey goodness' will make their specific patrons happy. Between them all, they've backed me into a corner. No, that's not quite right. I must say, rather, that they're all but backing me into four different corners at the same time!"

"So what are you going to do?"

"The only thing I can do. I've been given a second chance to make the Taft name mean something that Americans can be proud of—something that's a boon to my family, not a joke—and I think we all know that a third chance is quite unlikely. And time is in short supply. I can count the weeks to the Taft Party convention!"

"You don't have to tell me about the short supply of time." Her breathing had settled down into a steady, shallow rustle of the lungs. "Bill, I want you to promise me something."

"Yes, of course. Anything."

"Don't forget."

"I . . . I'll never forget you, Irene."

"No, not me, you dear man. Don't forget who you are. Don't forget where you come from. Where we come from. That America still exists. It's still here, underneath all this"—she waved her hand—"all this difficulty. Remember what made this a great nation, what made you a great man, in the first place."

"And what might that be?" asked Taft, a sad smile touching his face.

"Being you. Being yourself. All of us, from 1776 on. Reach into your heart. Do what you have to do, but don't let them turn you into someone else." She lightly rattled the tubes and wires that connected her body to the devices that kept her alive. "Don't let this century eat you up, President William Howard Taft. You eat it."

With that, she fell asleep. On his way out the door, Taft passed the incoming nurse. He glared at the man sternly, as if to reinforce the importance of the patient he was treating. But the only look he received in return was one of resignation and sympathy.

**FROM THE DESK OF REP. RACHEL TAFT
(Ind.–OH)**

Notes—Wed. 25th

—Plane lands at Reagan 7 a.m. Go straight to Capitol—full day of working the Hill to get more cosponsors for Int'l Foods Act.

—Do not take calls from campaign office. Remember why you're doing this. No point in forsaking the real work in order to boost ego delivering speeches to crowds.

—Grandpa can handle the Tafties for the next few weeks. I'll join back up at Taft Party National Convention in Cinci.

TWITTER—May 19, 2012

Robbrenner
Who caught the Taft speech in Pittsburgh yesterday? Man was on FIRE. #Taft #2012election

jamesjamesjames
@Robbrenner Yeah, it was incredible. He really doesn't hold back, does he? #Taft #2012election

tunabubbles
@Robbrenner @jamesjamesjames What was so great?

jamesjamesjames
@tunabubbles "The major part of a president's work is to keep tourists coming to town." Ha! Not cynical, just real talk. #Taft #2012election

tunabubbles
@jamesjamesjames LOL! I love those little Taftisms of his.

DarnPatriot
@jamesjamesjames @tunabubbles Jesus, you Tafties are starting to get even more pathetically sycophantic than the Ron Paul nuts. #TaftFail

jamesjamesjames
Suck it, @DarnPatriot. Taft is the most qualified candidate of the whole bunch. #Taft

tunabubbles

@Robbrenner @jamesjamesjames Either of you going to the Taft Convention?

Robbrenner

@tunabubbles We'll see. My unemployment checks stop next month and I still got nothing. Not the best time to fuss about with politics.

TWENTY-SIX

THE SPARSE PINES POKED through the lawns of the University of Cincinnati campus like wayward sentries, guardians of the past. Taft strolled along the mostly empty sidewalks; a few summer-semester students and faculty lingered in the humid evening air, and the energy of the recently departed spring semester had not entirely dissipated. But, for the most part, Taft had the place all to himself. Which suited him just fine.

He was recognized by most of the people on campus, of course. These were his hometown comrades, people who, long before he'd reawakened, were already constantly aware of the Taft family's historical prominence in Cincinnati, thanks to dozens of buildings and streets named for old Alphonso, Taft's father, as well as for himself. But when confronted by the living and breathing man, Taft's latter-day neighbors here, graciously, had the good sense and social parsimony to nod their heads respectfully before moving on. He was grateful.

It was that subtle, quiet, hometown affirmation Taft now sought out. Cicadas whispered in anticipation of the cool twilight as he wound his way toward the neoclassical stoicism of Blegen Library and toward the College of Law, a spot he felt both apt and flattering for the placement of the statue in his likeness.

He had to rub his eyes the first time he'd seen it, when he visited the campus with Susan at the start of the campaign as she consulted with a former colleague then tenured at UC. Not wanting to cause a stir, he'd drifted away from their historical discussion, wandering across the campus, the old Ohio sun as warm and friendly as ever on his face. He asked directions to the law school from a passerby, who looked at him with wide eyes before directing him on his way and then hurrying along.

He'd always felt a kinship to UC during his years teaching law here, despite being a Yalie through and through, and a member of Skull and Bones, no less, the covert fraternity his father had cofounded. Taft had never fully cottoned to the sneaky, elitist society, however, any more than he had the high office of the presidency and all its sordid secrets. But a law school, yes: that was the seat of his true brotherhood. That was where people were taught to lay truths and falsehoods out on the scales, to weigh and measure them against a body of precedent, to wield jurisprudence in interpreting the letter of the law.

After that first visit, he'd returned to the campus whenever he was able to take a few days away from campaigning to catch his breath in Cincinnati, as he did now. He snuck away at dusk, when it was easiest to shake off Kowalczyk's guard, and when it was less embarrassing to consult with the figure that now loomed before him.

His statue stood there, tucked away humbly enough at the rear entrance of the College of Law. At first he'd been angry that Susan hadn't told him about it, but then he realized she'd probably coaxed him here so that he'd discover it for himself. No matter. It was a weathered yet dignified effigy, one that depicted him—in slimmer days as a federal judge—dressed in his robes and holding a book, which is exactly how he'd always wished the world to picture him. Quiet, studious, fair, yet with a hint of easy geniality. That someone had seen fit to depict him this way, to cast him so in bronze, sent him over the moon. At least at first; as the summer, and the campaign, ground on, he'd begun to visit his statue more as a ritual, as a way of reminding himself of who he was, or at least who he felt he should be.

"Hello, old boy," he said aloud as he approached himself, the figure standing straight backed and staring out at the horizon. He sat down on the chipped edge of the dais and looked up at himself, the forced perspective almost comical to him. He patted the cool concrete of his perch. "How's your week been?"

The statue stared off, lost in bemusement.

"Oh, if only Susan could see me at this moment, talking to myself! The psychological depths she could plumb; she'd have a field day." He chuckled. "In any case, I may never have told you this, but I appreciate you keeping your guard up while I was, uh, underground for a few decades. It turns out the likeness is more durable than the man.

"Still, there's something to that, isn't there? You and I, we were both sculpted in someone else's image of us. It isn't a bad image. In many cases, it's kind of exaggerated for the better, don't you think? There you are, bold and upright and worthy of tribute, the way the sculptor chose to cast you. And there I was, a president of the United States . . . only my dear Nellie had to spend much of her life chipping away at the parts of me that were not a president. Maybe we're not so unlike, you and I. Ha, yes, well, of course we aren't, are we?"

The statue smiled silently.

"Of course, of course, old boy. Just grin and bear it. At least you get to hide out here at the rear entrance of a school you never attended. But there is one thing about you I don't envy." He tapped the dais. "Being tied down to this spot. Where would I be if I hadn't been able to run when the running was good? Then again, maybe being tied down would be a good thing for me. Not physically, of course. . . ." His speech trailed off as Rachel and Trevor and Abby and Susan all leapt to mind. He felt a sudden twinge of self-consciousness, but it only amused him further.

With those faces still dancing inside his head, Taft reached into his pocket. "In case I don't sound quite mad enough just talking at you, I also brought something for you." He pulled out a small, colorful plastic figure, Abby's Taft doll, the one she'd smuggled into his luggage before he'd left on his disastrous sabbatical with Kowalczyk. "I know two's company, but I figured why not make it a crowd?"

Whistling, he stood the little Taft on his tiny legs and began marching him around the base of the statue. Absurd, yes, he knew. But what wasn't absurd in this strange new life he'd been given?

He realized suddenly that he'd been whistling a song, "Come Josephine in My Flying Machine." He'd heard it only once since he woke up in this mad world: on the television at Rachel and Trevor's home, which had been showing a film, a love story, whose scenario was set amid the brief, tragic voyage of the *Titanic*.

The *Titanic*! It had been a disaster beyond belief in his time. It had sent the whole nation into mourning. It had taken away Taft's own best friend. But it was nothing compared to what the American of the twenty-first century dealt with almost daily. True, Americans today enjoyed more prosperity, better medical care, a higher standard of living, and far greater safety in almost every facet of life. But the potential for global catastrophe had increased alongside. What if he, miracle of miracles, ultimately won this election? Odds are, he'd be marching young men and women off to war with as much impunity as he was now marching his own small self around.

And then there was Irene. How long could she possibly hold on? And what would he do once that last link to his own time was severed? Susan probably knew at least as much about 1912 as Irene did, but Susan's soul was strictly academic. Or was it? Against his best judgment, he allowed himself to remember how she'd been nearly the first thing he thought of after waking up with Samantha on New Year's Day, and how he nonetheless shied away from acknowledging her presence in his life as not just a colleague but a woman. What was he so afraid of? That if he got too close, he'd once more let someone else dictate the proceedings of his life?

He patted the leg of the greater Taft. "What am I doing, worrying about these things?" he murmured. "No politician is his own man, nor should he be. He should be an implement of the people he represents. That's the problem, old boy, isn't it? *Who* am I potentially serving? Who are these Tafties, and why the hell do they think I can save them from themselves? Is it simply a case of everything old being new again? I guess I'll be finding out soon enough, at the convention." He snorted. "Taft Party National Convention, indeed. I've been trying to judiciously ration my speaking engagements since I announced my run—me, who was once taken to task regularly by the press for my long-winded speeches! But I can't face these people for more than a few minutes at a time before growing agitated. And it's certainly not as though I need to practice for the presidential debates. As a third-party crackpot, I won't even be asked to participate. Not that I regret no longer being a Republican; there's little left of the progressive party of mine to even recognize, let alone rally. And if my dealings with the GOP in 1908 and 1912 taught me anything, it's this: I don't want to be in any party that would have me as its leader." His face brightened, and he began rummaging through his pockets, looking for a pen and paper. "Hmm, that was a good one. I must jot that down!"

All he could find to write on was a wrapper. Some damned Fulsom confection or another. His stomach growled at the sight of it. He sighed. "Ah, yes, and then there's that, eh, my fellow Tafts? You two don't have to worry about it. The stuff you're each made of isn't elastic like this." He patted his belly, almost wistfully missing its insulating heft. "It seems the world today is full of this, this Fulsom-type garbage. We had candy and fatty foods in our day. And for a man of my admittedly secure if unostentatious means, I had access to as much of it as I could cram down my gullet. And cram I did. Oh, how they used to hound me about it! Everyone, from my family to the press to the common Cincinnatian. People, I daresay, are larger on average now than then. And yet, far more people diet and pay attention to nutrition today than in my time. I don't understand it. It's as if all these food products are designed specifically to addict folks to them. Why, as soon as I vowed to stop eating anything with the word *Fulsom* on it, among other things, it's as if my weight dropped magically. But what of the rest of the nation? Rachel is right. As loath as I am to grind government against commerce, some things just have to be regulated for the common good. It's not a trust, as we had to contend with back in our day, but it nonetheless needs busting. Or at least curbing.

"But enough about me! What do you think, fellows?" He wiggled the little Taft and then knocked a knuckle on the larger, which rang hollowly. "Speak up! Don't just go along with what I say. Let's argue the case like a good panel of judges, shall we? After all, haven't we aspired to the Supreme Court all our lives? Here we stand, before a school of law, inside of which is taught the history and rulings of that most august judicial body. How did we get so sidetracked, old boys? Weren't we on the fast track to appointment? Weren't we promised on more than one occasion that we'd get to that bench someday, if only we'd do just this one little task and that other little duty? The ultimate irony was the day I, as president, had to appoint my first Supreme Court judge. Me! Choosing the nominee and then handing over that honor to someone else. Not that Horace Lurton didn't wholly deserve it back in 1910. But then there was Hughes. And Van Devanter. And Lamar. And Pitney. Five! All said, I had to put five other men on that court. I would've given everything I owned, everything I'd ever accomplished, for the privilege of taking any one of their places. And yet, here is where I wind up. Running once more, for the third time, for an office I never aspired to in the first place. If ever there was proof that the Creator sneaks around behind our backs, hanging over our shoulders, pulling the strings of our fate for his own amusement. . . ."

Just then, Taft heard the soft fall of footsteps behind him. Then the clearing of a throat. He turned around to find what looked like a professor leaning toward him, as hesitantly as if approaching the last known specimen of a species thought to be extinct. "Sorry to interrupt you, sir, but . . . someone's been trying to call you on your cell phone." The woman took out a piece of paper from her pocket and read it. "Your, uh, granddaughter, Rachel. She contacted our office and asked that you call her immediately." Then she closed the paper and looked at him as directly as she was able. "I'm sorry to have to be the one to tell you this, Mr. Taft, but it seems a friend of yours has passed away. Irene Kaye? I'm so sorry."

With the action figure dangling between his fingers, Taft just stood there, as cold and immobile as the useless metal simulacrum above him.

The Cincinnati Journal
Obituaries
June 1, 2012

Irene Margaret Kaye Lived Through 19 Presidents, But Her Allegiance Belonged To One

Irene Margaret Kaye was a quiet woman with a kind smile. Her fellow residents at Patterson Senior Village will attest to that. She was by far the oldest resident of Patterson, and also one of the oldest residents of Ohio.

Mrs. Kaye died Monday, June 4, at Patterson Senior Village from complications arising from heart disease. She was 106.

Born Irene Margaret O'Malley to Irish immigrants and raised in the Hyde Park area, she was among the first 1,300 students enrolled at Withrow University High School in 1913, graduating in 1917. She married World War I veteran Joseph Kaye in 1920. They settled in Hyde Park and lived there their entire lives.

Mr. Kaye died in 1972 of diabetes, soon after the couple had sold their modest sewing shop and retired. Mrs. Kaye moved into Patterson Senior Village in 1981. Due to medical complications, the couple had no children. She is survived by various distant cousins.

Theodore Roosevelt was president of the United States when Mrs. Kaye was born, but her neighbors say she had always held a place in her heart for Roosevelt's successor, William Howard Taft.

"She loved to talk about the postcard she'd sent [Taft] when she was a little girl, back when he was still in office, before he disappeared and came back and all that," says Patterson head nurse Becky Shalom. "And, of course, Taft himself came to pay her a visit last fall, which delighted her to no end. She also collected teddy bears and made the most beautiful quilts you ever saw, but mostly she listened to other residents rather than talk about herself all the time. She was an angel."

Service will be held Friday, June 8, at Orlowitz Funeral Home. Burial will be in Walnut Hills Cemetery. —*Tracy Sullivan*

CLASSIFIED
Secret Service Incidence Report
BBR20120612.19
Agent Ira Kowalczyk

Attached find perimeter plan documents for 6/14, 6/15, and 6/16, the Taft Party National Convention at Great American Ball Park. Agents Pearsall, Horton, and myself assigned to Big Boy's personal detail; agents Mietus, Kerr, and St. John assigned to Grand Girl's. Have cleared all of Taft Party's hired security forces for general crowd-control duties.

At this point, my main concern is not any external threat to Big Boy's physical safety, but rather his psychological safety. He has been distracted and unfocused for the past two weeks. Must make sure he doesn't put himself in harm's way through sheer bloody Taftishness.

TWENTY-SEVEN

GREAT AMERICAN BALL PARK squatted at the south end of downtown Cincinnati, an overthrown pitch away from the Ohio River. Not that anyone was thinking about baseball today or, indeed, about anything other than the crowds. Taft had to hand it to the party leaders; they might not be—well, definitely were not—the campaign lieutenants he would have chosen had any of this been his own idea, but they nonetheless were capable organizers. As soon as the venue for the convention had been set in stone, they'd miraculously mobilized their various factions. Some anonymous benefactor had spent hundreds of thousands of dollars reserving every spare hotel room in the city and surrounding area. A fleet of private shuttles had shown up earlier in the week, ready to ferry battalions of Tafties from one event to the other. Umbrella-shaded food carts had popped up around the city like mushrooms, though Taft had noticed with a passing frown that the lunch vendors all seemed to carry a robust selection of Fulsom snacks among their wares. Wasn't anyone *listening* to him?

As ravenous as he was this morning, Taft sat in his makeshift office suite in the Millennium Hotel and ate as slowly as he could. Sharing breakfast helped; it was easier for him to avoid wolfing down an entire plate of food that way. Of course, the cardboard-like taste and texture of these newfangled whole-grain bagels slowed the process considerably. For the better, though; his diet hadn't been easy to institute and adhere to over the past few months. But what had been? Despite that he still needed to lose a good fifty pounds, he was on the mend; he let his momentary lapses—nights where he broke down and indulged in calories, carbohydrates, maudlin thoughts of Teddy and Nellie—pass behind closed doors, only to be forced to the back of his mind by morning.

He swallowed the last bite of his meager breakfast and pushed away the plate. He knew he should *feel* something. Anything. Here he was, arriving at a convention attended by thousands of people, all of them there to see and hear and support him. But today, like every day since Irene's funeral, he felt cold and hollow. Was he dead all over again? He thought he'd genuinely embraced his new life by joining this Taft Party campaign. But the knowledge that the last person he'd known from the past, however tenuous a link she may have been, was now gone, had left him irrevocably adrift in this century. He may as well have tossed his own soul into the grave with her, along with the Taft action figure he'd impulsively placed by her side in the casket while saying his final goodbyes.

And yet it wasn't just Irene. Nor was it just the overwhelming vertigo that came from trying to navigate the conflicting agendas of all these Taft Party patrons. Something, he felt, was askew. Unsettled. What was that saying Archie Butt had been so fond of, about waiting for the other boot to drop? That was the sensation Taft was experiencing, that he was hanging in an ill-defined limbo, failing to grasp some fundamental piece of the jumble that made up his existence.

Well, he thought, at least he'd been able to grow his mustache back to its full glory. He wouldn't have to stand in front of the assembled hordes of the Taft Party and recite his platform speech without the comfort of his luxurious twin tufts. That was something.

Not for the first time, he thanked the heavens that no one in the press had ever thought to refer to his whiskers as "Taft tufts." Or, at least, hadn't done so anyplace where he'd seen it. And then he sighed heavily as he remembered that, these days, even a child as young as Abby could likely use the Google to find fifty-three occurrences of that very formulation across eleven decades, without even trying very hard.

WELCOME TO THE 2012 TAFT PARTY NATIONAL CONVENTION MEDIA CENTER

Created by the 2012 Convention Host Committee in conjunction with the City of Cincinnati, this online pressroom provides media with ongoing news updates, access to hi-res images, and factual information about the host city.

FREQUENTLY ASKED QUESTIONS

Where did Taft dine and drink in his native Cincinnati, then and now? What's the best place to score Taft memorabilia? Where is the Party truly partying this weekend? We have the answers to all your questions regarding the big buildup to William Howard Taft's historic platform speech at Great American Ball Park on Saturday. // *Click for more.*

DEMS AND GOP CONSPICUOUS IN THEIR SILENCE
Friday, June 15, 2012

The Democratic and Republican leaderships—up to and including their parties' presidential candidates—surely have a strong opinion on the Taft Party National Convention. So why are they dodging questions and flagrantly ignoring it? Are they afraid—or *really* afraid? Cincinnati's best and brightest discuss the issue. // *Click for more.*

THANKS TO TAFT, HOT DOG CARTS GO GREEN
Friday, June 15, 2012

Many Taft conventioneers have been asking themselves a crucial question over the last two days: what's up with the hot dogs? Per William Howard Taft's explicit request, all twenty-two of Great American Ball Park's licensed hot dog vendors are now serving only organic, non-GMO veggie dogs for the duration of the TPNC. That's right: no meat. But what do the vendors—some of whom, like sausage vet Larry Welton, have been serving all-beef wieners at

Great American since the days of Riverfront Stadium—have to say about the switch? // *Click for more.*

CHICAGO PUNK BAND THE LOUSY KISSERS HOLD "FLASH CONCERT" IN FRONT OF GREAT AMERICAN BALL PARK
Friday, June 15, 2012

The first night of the Taft Party National Convention wound down with a series of speeches by Taft Party luminaries at Great American Ball Park. But the party was just getting started: a rowdy, inebriated, and by all accounts musically inept group called the Lousy Kissers pulled up to the ballpark's front entrance in the beds of two pickup trucks equipped with generators. Within moments, an equally unsavory crowd had formed around them—and the band's singer, later identified as Rob Reitman of Chicago, began screaming bawdy songs about Taft's allegedly legendary sexual exploits and the "piss-poor quality" of the veggie dogs the park had been serving all day. // *Click for more.*

The Taft 2012 Convention Daily—Friday

Delegate Spotlight: Why Taft, Why Now?

RAFAEL DELGADO, LOUISIANA: "When Taft was the governor general of the Philippines after the Philippine-American War, he refused to use the U.S. military to put down the Filipinos who kept resisting the occupation; instead, he trusted the local law officers to take care of it and gave them the support they needed. And it worked! Does that sound like a guy who'd, I don't know, say, get American forces stuck in Iraq for a decade? Because it doesn't to me. Taft 2012 all the way."

CHELSEA PENNYPACKER, CALIFORNIA: "He doesn't try to make stuff sound good for TV. He just talks. He doesn't care about getting good press, but he also doesn't try to shut the press out, and he doesn't waste time arguing with them. I can't remember the last time I saw a candidate who used so many polysyllabic words in the same press conference. Taft isn't afraid to be smart, but he also never sounds condescending."

MARIA JONES, MICHIGAN: "His first year in office, I guess, President Taft stuck his neck out to fire Teddy Roosevelt's favorite forestry officials when they couldn't get their act together and figure out how to work with the new bosses. I know at the time that Taft caught a lot of flak for it from the environmentalists, but I still like the fact that he cared enough to investigate the whole thing himself, instead of just accepting whatever either side told him. That reassures me that I could trust Taft to do what's right about the whole global-warming thing, because I know *I* sure can't figure out which scientists to listen to."

HERB YOUTIE, FLORIDA: "I'm a Republican because my father was a Republican, which means he would have voted for Taft in 1912. This is probably going to be the last election I'm around for, so I'm voting for Taft in 2012. Seems like the right thing to do."

Excerpts From Remote Surveillance Log, Great American Ball Park, Ground Floor, Men's Restroom 3, Urinals 7 and 8

Saturday, June 16, 12:56 p.m.

—There's still one thing I'm not totally sure about, though: Taft's stand on immigration.

—Yeah, I'll agree with you there. Seems like it's not his main focus. I sure know what I wish he would do about immigration, though.

—What's that?

—Just open the damn borders and charge money for citizenship.

—You're not serious?

—As a heart attack. Look, we waste how many billions of dollars trying to stop people from coming here? What's the point? I'm not even trying to get idealistic about it. I know America was built on immigration and all that, but that's not the point. I'm just being practical. If you can pay, you can come here. If you get caught without your receipt, you work it off until you can.

—Right. Like washing dishes if you can't pay your bill at the diner.

—Exactly.

—I'm truly impressed. I can't honestly tell if that's racist or not.

—See, that's why Taft is the man to do this. He was around before racism even existed, right? So he's in the clear.

—Um, I gotta go wash my hands.

Saturday, June 16, 3:49 p.m.

—I don't know if I can take another damn speech. Know what? Taft should outlaw political speeches. I mean it. Fuck 'em. Just a bunch of hot air. [*Subject eructates.*]

—Yeah, well, I don't know if I can take another one of those shitty plastic cups of Fulsom Lite. What do they brew that stuff with? Dishwater?

—Actually, I think you're looking at it.

TWENTY-EIGHT

"WHY, TAFT, OLD MAN, you're looking positively svelte."

The man who stood in the hotel hallway outside Taft's suite, speaking from around the back of Kowalczyk's shoulder, was tall, gray haired, and patrician, his flawlessly tailored suit accentuating the sharp lines of his nose and chin. Taft had never seen him before, though he knew the type: wealthy Northeasterners who wouldn't dream of carrying their pocket cash with anything other than solid-gold money clips.

"Wouldn't give me his name," said Kowalczyk, blocking the doorway, "but he's clean, and he says it's an urgent message from the party committee."

"That's about the size of it," the man said, stifling a yawn with an oddly contorted hand. Taft started as he recognized the twisted configuration of fingers. It was the secret greeting of the Taft family's old college legacy, the Skull and Bones Society. Taft was bemused to see his first face-to-face confirmation that the esoteric fraternity indeed still thrived, though of course they'd taken note of his reappearance and sent him that typically bizarre Christmas card. But what the devil could the man possibly be pestering him for, a mere three hours before he was scheduled to address the whole of the Taft Party National Convention from its main stage?

"My good fellow," Taft said, "I do appreciate your solicitousness, but I am—I am rather thoroughly occupied today! Why don't you leave me your calling card, and we shall schedule a meeting when I might devote the proper attention."

"Of course," said the man in the suit, smiling faintly, and withdrew a card from his breast pocket. Taft took it and had already opened his mouth to bid the man farewell when the name on the card registered in his vision: AUGUSTUS FULSOM. Taft's mouth hung open as he stared from the card back to the man, who nodded silently.

"Kowalczyk," Taft said, "this gentleman and I will speak privately for a moment. Do let any other callers know that I'm unavailable until after the speech, yes?" Ignoring the bodyguard's quizzical look, he gestured for Fulsom to enter the room and closed the door behind them.

"Good to see a brother Bonesman back on his feet, Taft," Fulsom said, seating himself upon the desk by the window overlooking the river view. "Ah, Cincinnati. Beautiful city. Did you know that Cincinnati has one of the highest per-capita rates of Fulsom Foods products in the Midwest? And for the Midwest, that's saying something."

"One of the highest obesity rates, too," Taft answered. He drifted to the coffee table in front of the sofa and nonchalantly flipped over his open notebook. "Not to mention diabetes, heart disease, and colon cancer, *and* the industrial runoff from the three Fulsom plants in the vicinity."

"Plants   that   employ   approximately   two   thousand

Cincinnatians, if I remember correctly," Fulsom said. "In a recession, no less."

"I think it might be best, sir, if you explained your visit," Taft said stiffly. "Surely you are aware from my public comments that I am not a supporter of your company's work."

"What, that?" Fulsom waved a hand casually, as if to brush the remark aside. "That's nothing to worry about, Taft. We all have the game to play. I don't take it personally."

"Game? You think I play mere politics, sir? You foist unwholesome foods upon the American people, and I shall continue to say so."

Fulsom arched an eyebrow. "Everything is politics, and there's nothing 'mere' about it. Take this campaign of yours. It's a lark. It's a carnival show. You're playing the role of the jolly jester who's allowed to say silly things because you've got a silly mustache and a silly belly. And yet you're winning the hearts of Americans left and right. Crazy as it sounds, Taft, you just might take this election."

It was a thought Taft had been refusing to think. "And?"

"And whether you do or not, I'm on your side. I'm behind you, William Howard Taft. Because we Bonesmen have got to stick together. Eight years ago—before your time, I know—we had two Bonesmen going at each other for the White House, the Republican and the Democrat both, and it was ugly. Not the race—that's always ugly—but the rift it caused in Skull and Bones, half the membership taking sides against the other half. Ruined Christ knows how many perfectly good business partnerships just because people took their politics personally. I'm not about that. I want to see the wheels of commerce keep on spinning smooth as ever. And that means never mind what you say about me in public. What matters is, behind closed doors, we all know that we're lending each other a hand."

Taft's lip curled in disgust as he remembered the last two times he'd *done business* with Fulsom Foods behind closed doors: in Rachel's bathroom after Thanksgiving dinner and in the obscene food factory of Atomizer restaurant. "I hope you'll forgive me for saying so, Fulsom, but Bonesmen or not, I generally prefer to choose my own intimates, and I specifically prefer to decline this 'helping hand' of yours, thank you."

"Well," Fulsom murmured, "it's a bit late for that, don't you think?"

The smug confidence of the man's tone made Taft more nervous than he cared to admit. "Pardon me?"

"Oh, Taft. You big, innocent Taft of a man. Do you really think all these little Taft Party clusters around the country just willed themselves into being on a wing and a prayer? Do you think the poll numbers move themselves? Where do you think Osborne got the money to pull together so many Southern Christians, Eldridge got the money to assemble all those malcontent Republicans and Libertarians, Lommel got the money to convince entire trade unions to consider an alternative to the Democratic Party?"

"From . . . citizens' groups," Taft said, and he could hear the sound of sick revelation in his own voice. There, he supposed, was that other boot dropping at last.

"Sure. One citizen's groups. Mine. What you had, Taft, was a bunch of fans around the water cooler and on the Internet. I made sure they got enough money and support to turn themselves into a Taft Party. This whole convention? You're welcome. Consider it a welcome-back bash."

Taft's mind scrambled furiously to make sense of it. This was madness. If there was one, *single* thing he'd never do with his reputation, with his good name, it was ally with the forces of an amoral sick-monger like Fulsom, who doubtless saw men and chickens alike as only so much meat to be pureed and reshaped. But the sinking pit in his stomach assured him that, madness though it might be, it was also the truth. He'd encountered many men like Fulsom during his years in government—men who found their own worth only by controlling the fates of others—but he'd always held a sure enough footing to avoid being tripped up by their manipulations. But now he was in an unfamiliar world, and he'd allowed his disorientation to make him a target—a big, fat target, he thought bitterly.

And yet, he thought, it couldn't be that simple. Something wasn't right. "Why on earth," he said, "would you want me, Bonesman or not, back in the White House, using the bully pulpit to denounce your infernal sausage grinder of a company?"

Fulsom slid to his feet. "Think about it, Taft," he smiled. "For God's sake. You're a big boy." He walked to the door, put his hand on the knob, and paused. "Oh, and about that. Congratulations on your diet. But don't lose too much weight, now. You're a brand, Taft. A valuable brand. Just like Fulsom." Then he slipped out the door quietly, leaving Taft to his privacy.

Taft sat perfectly still, unmoving, for fifteen minutes, then twenty, then twenty-five, as the threads of yet another new reality wove themselves into a pattern he could comprehend.

Blast it all, he hadn't asked to be in this damnable position. Had he? He had. He had felt so lost in this strange new world, so helpless, that he had seized upon the first opportunity to make a grand assertion of potency. His granddaughter, the Tafties—he'd seen a way to help them, he thought, and thus to prove his life still had meaning. And so he'd hurled himself right back into the very campaign trail he'd been so eager to walk away from, just a year and a hundred earlier.

And, if he was to be honest with himself, he hadn't just done it for them, either.

He looked over at his desk, where several stacks of books and papers were piled three layers high. A particular manila folder sat at the bottom of the tallest stack. All right, he thought violently, it was well nigh time to stop hiding from the past. He jerked himself to his feet before he could change his mind and pulled out the folder where Susan had gathered all the records of his apparent death. He brushed his hand across the photo of Nellie, then shuffled the papers below it and pulled out the eulogy Teddy Roosevelt had delivered at his funeral.

He read it. And then he sat still for five more minutes.

He rose again and went to tell Rachel what had transpired, and to suggest to her what they should do about it. He knew she would agree. But he had to give her the chance to disagree. She was, after all, her own woman.

But he knew she would agree. She was, after all, a Taft.

From *Taft: A Tremendous Man*, by Susan Weschler:

When I first set out to study William Howard Taft's life and presidency, one question presented itself over and over again: how did he ever get to the White House? Taft hated the dirty business of politics. Hated the sorts of people who care about holding power. Hated lies, little white ones or otherwise. And, as far as I could tell, he hated it when people didn't like him. Because he loved to be able to agree with people, to find common ground with them.

Finally I realized: I, like most of those who'd known him, had underestimated him. Taft was modest and agreeable, but he wasn't milquetoast. And he wasn't lacking in ambition, either. The closer I examined the turning points of his résumé, the more certain I was that, often, he let those around him think they were leading him around when, in fact, the opposite was true. That's not to say he was manipulative—it seemed entirely possible that he didn't even realize he was doing it—but he became president because he'd always put himself in a place where his decency would get noticed. Noticed, rewarded, and relied upon. That, in and of itself, was a kind of ruthlessness.

Who knows what might have happened if Taft hadn't vanished in 1913? How might he have turned his reelection defeat around—turned losing the presidency into an eventual triumph for himself and the principles by which he lived?

Tantalizing as the question may be, we can never know the answer to how Taft's twentieth century might have been different. We can only know what happened in the twenty-first.

Transcript, *Raw Talk with Pauline Craig*, broadcast June 16, 2012

PAULINE CRAIG: Welcome to a very special edition of *Raw Talk with Pauline Craig*. Viewers, just a few short months ago, *Raw Talk* brought you the nation's first live, one-on-one conversation with former president William Howard Taft. Since then, I've made sure you've had a front-row seat to what just might be the most important political phenomenon of our generation: the birth of a new party, inspired by the rebirth of a great American. The Taft Party has quickly become a remarkable juggernaut on the campaign trail, though both the Democratic and Republican parties have done their best to ignore it, to pretend everything is just business as usual. Well, I can tell you, everything is *not* business as usual. Especially not today. Today, anticipation among the Tafties is at an all-time fever pitch, as the thousands assembled in Cincinnati wait for William Howard Taft to deliver his keynote address to the Taft Party National Convention, just two short hours from now. Over the past week, we've seen the poll numbers take a remarkable curve, as significant numbers of previously undecided voters now say they're planning to vote Taft. And if today's Internet search trends are any indicator, come tomorrow the major party candidates are finally going to have to stand up and admit that the Taft factor is real, it's massive, and it's not going away anytime soon.

FROM THE DESK OF REP. RACHEL TAFT
(Ind.–OH)
Notes—Sat. 16th

—Well. Fun while it lasted.

—Remember we were never going to win anyway.

—Prepare for the shit to hit the fan.

—Pray to all things holy that Wm Howard can announce this to the Tafties without getting crucified. Without getting us all crucified.

—No whining. No whining. No whining. Back to work on Monday.

"WE DO NOT KNOW what has become of our vanished friend, William Howard Taft. We pray that his soul has found peace. And I, myself, pray for forgiveness. Taft has been the kindest, gentlest, fairest man I have been privileged to know and work alongside in all my years serving these United States of America. In recent times, I have not echoed his goodness. During these past two years I have called him a weak president; I have called him a traitor to my own presidency; I sought to muscle my way back into the office I had left to him. I was behaving a brute, and I shall regret it for the rest of my days. William Taft has been my friend and my brother; yet, when I perceived that his actions and principles as president were diverging from my own, I permitted my righteous indignation to drive me against him—and that was the true betrayal. That was the true failure: my failure to support a devoted comrade, even as he struggled to act his own man. Sir, wherever you are today, know that I most bitterly curse myself for allowing our friendship, and your last days, to fall victim to my vanity. Could I now undo my folly, I would. William Howard Taft, the world deserved your presence longer."

—*Former president Theodore Roosevelt,*
delivering his eulogy for William Howard Taft, 1913

TWENTY-NINE

WILLIAM HOWARD TAFT had been a boy playing ball on the streets of Cincinnati; a young man in love with a brilliant, heartbreakingly lovely woman; a judge and a governor charged daily with making decisions that would shape the lives of hardworking people, for better or worse; and, finally, the inhabitant of one of the most powerful offices in the world. And as he walked onto the stage to the relentless, booming wave of applause that struck him in the chest even as the blinding spotlights smote him in the eyes, what he thought was: well, it has all come to this.

He raised his hand and, incredibly, the cheering surged louder. No, that wouldn't do at all. He waved sharply, once, in the abrupt chopping motion he'd learned through years of necessity, and slowly the crowd quieted. Taft cleared his throat.

"My friends," he said. "My fellow Americans."

He paused.

"They say that the cheerful loser is a sort of winner. I am well accustomed to this perspective!" There was widespread laughter.

"Today . . . today I am a winner, indeed. For today I face the prospect of the greatest loss I could ever experience. And I find that I am possessed of the surest, most certain, and indeed the most cheerful peace of mind any man could possibly have.

"I do not speak of the election. The election—and I will be blunt now, and I dare say you will be startled, but fear not, for this is a simple truth which at heart I know you all understand—the election is a small thing." Now there was near-total silence. "Men and women win and lose elections every year, and they perform to the best of their abilities, or sometimes to the worst of their corruptions, and the nation goes about its business. It is true that some presidents, some congressmen, some judges are better than others; some are worse. It is true that some face unthinkably great challenges and rise to the occasion, while others manage to bungle affairs that should have been handled by a competent statesman with the simplest of ease. And yet the nation goes on, so long as every new election arrives and we resolve to do it again, and to do it right. To once more choose the finest candidate we can find. It is not any one election that matters. It is *all* the elections, together, in a continuum that ensures we will never rest upon our laurels but will strive anew for constant betterment.

"I have been proud to serve this nation once as its president. As you know, my work in that office was difficult, and I cannot honestly say that I enjoyed it, but it was important work—work that, some days, meant fighting to make sure the right men were safeguarding our nation's forests and, some days, meant fighting against those who would abuse their wealth to harm those less privileged than themselves and, other days, meant fighting against some of my dearest friends in all the world! Because I believed they had made decisions that were wrong for the American people. I lost those friends because of the work I did as president, and although it was, frankly, an awful time, I can say to you with a clear conscience that I would do it again. Because being president, above all, was work that I was *called to do*, and I have never been one to brush off a call from those who need me."

Applause burst out again, but Taft waved it down. "*You* have called me here, and I have answered. But today an even greater call has come, and I stand here now to deliver my answer."

For an instant he held his breath. And then, stroking his mustache, he thought, to hell with it, and took a bold step across the Rubicon. "Three hours ago, Rachel and I discovered that the largest donations to the Taft Party USA came from so-called citizens groups that are, in fact, no such thing but mere fronts for the largest food-production conglomerate in the Western hemisphere, Fulsom Foods International."

A buzz of murmuring and confused head-swiveling burst through the assemblage. Taft allowed it to propagate for a few moments before continuing. "As you know, during this campaign I have made no secret of my distaste for the supposedly edible products that Fulsom stamps out in its factories and foists upon the American marketplace under the guise of nutrition. Naturally, I was alarmed and dismayed—to say the very least!—to learn that I had been the benefactor of that very company's largess.

"At first, I pridefully believed that Fulsom had surreptitiously funded the Taft effort because he—Augustus Fulsom, the man at the top—wanted me to be president. My own self-love may not be as hugely robust as is my waistline, but a political campaign will make any man believe great things of himself. And thus I thought that Fulsom wanted to take advantage of my new popularity by placing a man in the White House who would be indebted to him. It occurred to me that a new Taft presidency particularly would serve Fulsom well in that regard, even should I continue to rail against his firm's abominations, because, let us be honest: when it comes to food, I am known as a man who allows my appetite to overrule my self-discipline. And in this television-fueled, Internet-soaked era of 2012, no matter what healthy policies I might pursue, the very picture of my—well, my rotundity—seated behind the desk in the Oval Office would send a message to all that America is a nation of constant eating.

"That, as I say, was my first thought. I believe it was the thought Fulsom wished me to have. But then I had another, and immediately cursed myself for a fool.

"Moneyed interests such as Fulsom do not back third parties because they expect us to win. They do *not* expect us to win. Indeed, they and their fellows spend countless sums each year to ensure that the familiar sway of partisan politics will continue as always. And so I asked myself: why in heaven's name should Fulsom fund the Taft Party, if not to put me back into the White House?

"The answer, my dear friends, presented itself along with the question. For you all have called yourselves the Taft Party. Not the William Howard Taft Party, just the Taft Party. And there is a second Taft here to consider, is there not? My running mate, my granddaughter, the very fine representative from the state of Ohio, Rachel Taft." He gestured to the side of the stage, letting the crowd look to where Rachel stood, hands clasped behind her back like a soldier at ease, the very picture of resolved dignity. "She is not the celebrity I have become since my strange rebirth. No, she is simply and utterly an honest, dedicated, patriotic, unimpeachable legislator who has devoted her life to doing good work for her country, for the future in which her daughter shall someday grow up.

"And her chosen cause is not one that Fulsom finds acceptable.

"Rachel Taft—as you will know if you have been following our campaign this season—is the sponsor of the new International

Foods Act currently winding its way through House committees and subcommittees. This bill, a thorough updating of the regulations that today guide the nation's food industry, would hold corporations such as Fulsom responsible for the consequences of their practices, particularly the sorts of practices that had yet to be invented when the laws were last written.

"My friends, when I arrived here in your time, I became a fast patron of the unthinkably vast and colorful array of meats, treats, and sweets I found in your kitchens and dining establishments." That was a clever turn of phrase, he quietly congratulated himself, noting the rhyme for future reuse. "I enjoyed your Twinkies and your take-out, and I even enjoyed a flavorful Thanksgiving dinner . . . until the innards of my Fulsom TurkEase disagreed most profoundly with my own innards, which come from an age of simpler cuisine. I wholly understand the great achievements of the modern agricultural business; the food they produce is both endlessly bountiful and incredibly affordable for even the humblest of Americans, so that every family may enjoy a full stomach. Truly, this seems a divine blessing we enjoy today, living in a world of plenty that can satiate all our hungers.

"And yet . . .

"And yet at the base of it, it is a false bounty, a cornucopia that cannot endure happily. For there are lies mixed in at the bottom of the bowl, so to speak.

"I do not even speak of the unsavory practices involved in the processing of these foodstuffs: the reconstitution of grains into approximations of meats, of meats into facsimiles of grains, of sugars into every other consumable that can possibly be imagined. Nor, by the same token, do I mean to belittle the individual Americans who work so hard every day to bring it to bear. Quite the opposite! The welfare of the farmer is vital to that of the whole country. Rather, it is the entire structure that surrounds the farmer and the grocer and the gourmet that gives me concern.

"If there is a problem with America today—as I see it—it is that we look for self-worth in consumption, rather than in the pursuit of personal achievement. I may seem a hypocrite for pointing such a finger, for I have obviously engaged in quite a bit of overconsumption myself! Nonetheless, it is true. We cannot fill the void in our souls by stuffing ourselves with physical comforts; we can fill it only by striving to achieve excellence. That noble goal holds different specifics for each of us. Where one American may become an excellent doctor or lawyer or taxicab driver, another may become an excellent mother, and yet another an excellent golfer!

"We all possess excellence within us from the start. For excellence is not a measure to be taken against others; it is a measure to be taken against oneself. The pursuit of achievement does not mean that one is a failure if he isn't the acknowledged leader in his field; it is not a question of outperforming others. It is a matter of performing *alongside* others! Excellence is something we can all share as Americans and, more fundamentally still, as human beings."

Somewhere out in the sea of humanity that faced him, Taft heard an angry voice cry: "Socialism!"

He harrumphed. "No, sir, it is most assuredly not the practice of socialism that I advocate. I must be so bold as to ask: are you quite certain you grasp what socialism truly is? I am talking about something quite different: simple self-respect."

Taft sighed. "These tremendous forces that crash against us from above, these monoliths of habit and government and industry and pure social momentum can make it difficult to afford oneself the respect that every person deserves. We cannot pretend *not* to know how small each of us seems compared to the colossus of a world-spanning corporation whose name is found in every corner market—compared to the juggernaut of an election whose every twist and turn is blared, all day long, every day, all year, from all the televisions and newspapers and Twitters and Googles!

"These relentless, unstoppable institutions, larger than any one American yet lacking the basic human compassion that we, each of us, possess—that, my friends, that is the sort of thing I fought against when I was president. It is the sort of thing that Teddy Roosevelt, God rest his soul, looked so heroic fighting against, which indeed is why I agreed to run for president in 1908 in the first place. I thought I could continue pushing Teddy's good fight forward. But I have discovered something about heroic struggles that many would-be heroes never grasp: acts of greatness are not singular acts. They are made up of many small acts that, taken one at a time over long years, do not look terribly heroic at all.

"Just take Teddy himself. Theodore Roosevelt spent years achieving relatively small feats in an escalating series of steps forward as a leader of men—as an officer in the United States Army, as a participant in the conservation movement, even as governor of New York. Finally, he possessed the ability to take the ultimate reins of leadership as president. At which point, he was able to turn around and delegate to others so many of the small acts that he would add up to a great president. I know this truth firsthand, for I was one of those doers of Teddy's small things! I left my judicial appointment to work in the Philippines under his direction; I went to Panama to get construction under way on the canal when a calm hand was required; I took responsibility of administering the War Department when a new man was called for. Were these great tasks? Certainly not; they were simply tasks that needed doing, and I was proud to do them for a man who knew how all the pieces of the puzzle fit together. Indeed, I was so proud to be one of Teddy's extra limbs, as it were, and I so admired the work he did in marshaling us all that I allowed myself to be convinced I could take his place when his term was ended."

Taft caught his breath again. He had no idea how long he'd been standing there speaking. They were all still staring at him, rapt.

"But that was Teddy's excellence," he said. "I, myself, am a different beast. The small acts of my own life, as I grew into a man, were not the acts of a commander but, rather, the acts of a judge. I was a good judge! Surely I heard thousands of cases, through all of which I listened to Americans of all sorts attest to the central facts and conflicts of their lives, and I strove mightily to return their testimony with fair, careful, thoughtful decisions. That, if I may say so, is my excellence. I am an excellent judge.

"It did not," he added slowly, articulating every word, "make me a great president."

In his peripheral vision, just behind Rachel at the platform's edge, he saw Susan Weschler brush her hand across her eyes.

"Teddy was a great president," Taft said. "But here is my question. What about his daughter? Did you know that Teddy had a brilliant spitfire of a daughter, Alice? Oh, she was a force to be reckoned with, that one! All the genius and force of will that made Teddy a figure worth carving into the side of a mountain multiplied threefold and bursting from the seams of a scowling little girl! Yes, Alice spent her White House years in a constant tornado, bursting into Cabinet meetings to yell at her father, outsmarting her bodyguards on a daily basis, literally climbing the walls to spend the night on the roof doing heaven knows what. She was a Roosevelt to the very core, a hero waiting to happen, and you would think that—surely!—she would be the centerpiece of Teddy's life, his prize possession. But do you know what he told a reporter one day when Alice flew through the office to interrupt their interview? 'I can be the president of the

United States,' he said, 'or I can attend to being Alice's father, but I cannot possibly do both.'

"I . . . I cannot be that great a president. It is not *the people*, in the abstract, who most move me; it is *people*. Real people. People like those I met in the courtroom, who looked me in the eye and told me their troubles. People like my great-great-granddaughter, Abby, who may be an Alice Roosevelt herself someday, searching for a way to find her own excellence, and whom I will surely attend to first and foremost when that day comes! And people like my . . . my great-granddaughter, Rachel, whose excellence stands manifest before the world already.

"It is for Rachel's excellence, above all, that I must assess all these matters and announce to you now the only decision that is fair and right, the decision I would make were I a judge listening to my own story, the decision that Rachel and I made together not long before I stepped out here before you: the Tafts must withdraw from our candidacy in this election."

Furious rumbling erupted all around, and once more Taft held up his hand. "We should not have entered the race in the first place, had we known that the good people of the Taft Party had been unknowingly propped up by the coffers of Fulsom Foods. Rachel Taft has a mission in Congress, and it is a noble one: to craft laws that will help safeguard and protect the well-being of the American people. If we were to remain in the race, she would be beholden to the business interest most deeply affected by her own legislation!—and had we not announced our discovery of this fact now, then, when it inevitably came to light in the months ahead, her credibility would be forever tainted. No, the true work of good, honest government is more important than any one presidential campaign, than any one old politician—more important even, though it pains me to say, than the name Taft itself."

He looked out across the field of Tafties, seeing a strange mix of dismay and approval there. "I am humbled," he said, "by the support you have shown me. Your enthusiasm is infectious—so much so, in fact, that I must remember not to allow it to warp my best judgment! I say this to you now: my withdrawal, once and for all, from the realm of presidential politics may seem a cause for campaign-season mourning; but in fact I believe it is the greatest opportunity that the women and men of the Taft Party could possibly have. For reason and fairness and honesty and free thinking—the fundamental principles of our platform—are admirable traits that belong to all Americans, from all across the wide canvas of the political and social spectrum. These things are not limited *just* to conservatives, or *just* to liberals, or *just* to rural or urban or suburban folk!

"We must pursue them and treasure them together as a whole people. And so I challenge you today, my friends, my neighbors, to cease projecting your hopes and dreams onto me alone— onto any one single leader!—and instead to turn this Taft Party into something bigger than me, bigger even than the presidency. I challenge you to build it into an ongoing, sustainable effort encouraging *all* Americans to seize their towns, their states, their country by the horns—together!—and make of it what they will. That party would be a party worth holding."

As he heard his own words, a wild idea entered Taft's head, and he was unable to prevent the grin from spreading across his face. "That party," he said, "should not be named for me. Nor should it be named for any man at all, but for an idea. If indeed we are to seize America by the horns, then we should do so under a horned banner. I say, let us call this grand movement of 2012 and beyond . . . the new Bull Moose Party!"

Scattered cheers mixed with laughter mixed with a hazy fog of confusion. Well, Taft thought, at least some of them understand me, and that will have to be good enough.

"We are all imperfect," he said, remembering a speech he'd given years before. "And so we cannot expect perfect government. The president cannot make the clouds rain or the corn grow, nor can he make business good; although when these things occur, political parties do claim some credit for the good things that have happened in this way." He wiped a hand across his sopping brow. "As I look back as far in my memory as I can, to my youth in the 1870s, and think of what has progressed in the inventions of the human race, the changes are marvelous. The telephone, the motorcar, the electric lifestyle—the airplane, the television, the Google, even the digital golf course!—what would we do without them? How rapidly we adapt ourselves to feel the absolute *necessity* of those improvements, of which we knew and imagined nothing a mere hundred fifty years ago! And yet many of these are only conveniences or comforts. True necessities confront us from other directions: the fuel to power all these devices, for one, and the fuel to healthily power our own bodies, for another.

"And now—my friends!—do not let us minimize the task before us. We Americans are a good people—a very, very good people—but one of our weaknesses is an assumption, justified by a good many miracles that have saved us from egregious mistakes in the past, that we should always expect America to be healthy and strong on its own, because we believe that God looks after children, drunken men, and the United States! We must get beyond that assumption. I do not know how we will do so. But I know we must.

"It has been," Taft concluded, "an honor and a privilege, albeit an unexpected one, to carry your banner thus far. I cannot continue waving it at your vanguard, but you have my promise that I shall always offer you whatever small good my quiet, humble contributions may possibly be worth in the future." And then he bowed at the waist and walked down the steps at the side of the stage, where Rachel and Susan embraced him. The applause was loud, though possibly not as loud as before.

"That," said Rachel, "was some speech."

"That?" said Taft. "Pshaw! I have delivered longer." He thought for a moment. "Though not, I will grant you, without writing them down first."

EPILOGUE
2021

THIRTY

"HEREBY DO I, William Howard Taft, solemnly affirm that I will administer justice without respect to persons, and do equal right to the poor and to the rich, and that I will faithfully and impartially discharge and perform all the duties incumbent upon me as a justice of the Supreme Court under the Constitution and laws of the United States. So help me God."

 —*William Howard Taft, speaking the traditional oath at his swearing-in ceremony as justice of the Supreme Court, as administered by President Rachel Taft, March 2021*

ACKNOWLEDGMENTS

This book would not exist without the aid of numerous research texts, but two in particular: *The William Howard Taft Presidency* by Lewis L. Gould (which taught me what kind of president Taft was) and *William Howard Taft: An Intimate History* by Judith Icke Anderson (which taught me what kind of man Taft was). That said, any distortion of Taft's character or accomplishments is wholly mine. And probably on purpose.

As for a bottomless well (pit?) of inspiration, I owe everything to our collective benefactor, bogeyman, savior, and specter: the American two-party political system. Long may she waver.

Mostly, though, I'd like to express my everlasting gratitude to my editor, Stephen H. Segal. *Taft 2012* was his mad idea, and his patience, passion, and inspired input made it all possible. Thanks, Stephen, for letting me babysit your brainchild. This book is as much yours as it is mine.

ABOUT THE AUTHOR

JASON HELLER is a journalist, author, and editor whose work has appeared frequently in *The A.V. Club*, *Alternative Press*, *Weird Tales*, *Fantasy Magazine*, *Clarkesworld*, Tor.com, and numerous papers in the Village Voice Media chain. He is the author of *The Captain Jack Sparrow Handbook* (2011) and a contributor to the *A.V. Club* book *Inventory* (2009). *Taft 2012* is his first novel. He lives in Denver, Colorado.